7<u>th</u> Heaven™

MARY'S STORY

Based on the hit TV series
created by Brenda Hampton

Based on teleplays and stories by Brenda Hampton
and Greg Plageman and Linda Ptolemy

Random House  New York

All rights reserved under International and Pan-
American Copyright Conventions. Published in the
United States by Random House, Inc., New York,
and simultaneously in Canada by Random House of
Canada Limited, Toronto.

Library of Congress Catalog Card Number: 99-64375
ISBN: 0-375-80332-7

Printed in the United States of America
November 1999
10 9 8 7 6 5 4 3 2

RANDOM HOUSE and colophon are registered trademarks
of Random House, Inc.

O N E

"Just what did you do with my cheerleader uniform?" Lucy Camden demanded of her older sister, Mary. "It was hanging on the door five minutes ago."

"Yeah, and blocking our only mirror!" Mary replied.

"Oh, I'm *so* sorry!" Lucy cried. "Now where did you put it?"

Mary shrugged. "I hung it in your closet," she said.

It was the morning "rush hour" at the Camdens'. As usual, traffic was heavy in the hallway, on the stairs, and around the upstairs bathroom. Things were even more hectic than usual because today was Friday. Fridays always meant after-school activities.

Today, Lucy had cheerleading practice, Mary was going to shoot hoops, and Simon had a class project due.

Lucy ripped open the closet door and snatched her uniform off the hook. It was still in its dry-cleaning bag. Lucy laid the outfit flat across her bed, which—unlike Mary's—was already made.

"You'd better get moving," Lucy said as she pulled the plastic wrapping off her uniform. "We're going to be late again."

"And we have to drive Simon to school today. Dad has an appointment."

"Great!" Lucy moaned. "I could barely get up this morning. I hardly slept last night with the babies crying."

The girls' new brothers were only a few weeks old. But sometimes Lucy felt as if they'd been keeping her awake for years.

Mary began to load her gym bag. Lucy dried her blond hair with a towel.

"All ready to go," Mary announced with a flourish. "How about you?"

Lucy, still dressed in her bathrobe, glared at her sister. She'd spent most of the morning cleaning up her side of the room while Mary dominated the shower.

But before Lucy could reply, the phone on the nightstand rang.

The second line had been installed recently, and Lucy and Mary loved it. It gave both of them the kind of privacy they'd never experienced.

But the extra line was also an extravagance since the arrival of the twins. Their parents had insisted that the second line had to go by the end of the month.

Lucy sighed as she reached for the phone. It would be a terrible loss.

She immediately recognized the voice on the other end of the line. Her mouth dropped open in surprise.

"It's for you," Lucy said, and thrust the phone into Mary's hands.

Matt sat at the kitchen table, hunched over a notepad. He heard the phone ringing upstairs, but chose to ignore it. It was probably for Lucy or Mary, anyway.

Let one of them *answer it,* Matt decided. He had other things on his mind.

He was clutching a pen in one hand and a mug filled with tea in the other.

Between sips, Matt scribbled furiously across the notepad. He hardly noticed the words he was writing. They weren't important, anyway. They were just random thoughts.

Whenever Matt was locked inside a problem, he tried to put his ideas down on paper. Usually, writing things down led him to a solution.

But today it didn't seem to be working.

Matt sighed and wrote down a few more notes. Still no good. He ran a hand through his long, straight hair in frustration.

Just then, the doorbell rang.

Matt pretended he hadn't heard it.

"Good morning!" his younger sister Ruthie warbled as she entered the kitchen. She sighed and plopped down in a chair across the table from her brother.

"We have company," she announced. "Maybe someone should answer the door. That would be the *polite* thing to do."

"Mom'll get it," Matt said.

"I guess so." Ruthie shrugged. "If she can get away from those two screaming brats, anyway."

Matt set down his tea and went back to his scribbling. Ruthie watched her brother with genuine curiosity. While he wrote, she pulled at her dark brown ringlets and fidgeted in her chair.

Finally, Ruthie sighed theatrically.

Matt continued to ignore her.

When Ruthie was sure she'd get no attention from her oldest brother, she took a cereal bowl from the center of the table and a spoon from the rack.

With one finger on her chin, Ruthie reviewed the line of cereal boxes on the shelf. She made her selection and brought the box back to the kitchen table.

As the kernels of crisp roasted corn piled slowly into her bowl, Ruthie glanced at her brother. When she poured the milk, she cleared her throat loudly.

Matt continued to write.

Ruthie sat down again and stared at her brother, willing him to notice her. But Matt wrote on, locked in concentration.

Ruthie gazed up at the ceiling. "Am I invisible?" she asked no one in particular.

Matt looked at his sister from behind a curtain of hair. "I'm busy, Ruthie…okay?"

"So is Mom," Ruthie complained. "And Dad *and* even that rat Simon."

"Where are Mary and Lucy?" Matt asked, his eyes still on his notepad.

"They're on the phone!" Ruthie crossed her arms.

"Both of them?"

"Well, Mary is on the phone," Ruthie elaborated. "Lucy only answered it for her."

"I see."

"Mary is talking to a boy," Ruthie added, hoping that piece of news would interest Matt. But he had already returned to his work.

Ruthie suddenly realized her cereal was getting soggy. She decided to stop hounding her brother for now and eat.

He's sure been acting strange since he started college, Ruthie told herself as she chewed on the sweet, not-so-crunchy cereal.

In the foyer, Mrs. Camden answered the door.

Matt started on a fresh sheet of paper. His own breakfast—toast, a glass of milk, and an apple—sat untouched at his elbow. Matt stared glumly at the sloppy writing. It still wasn't making any sense.

Ruthie leaned across the table and read the words Matt had written.

"Rich man, poor man, beggar man, thief," she said. *"Doctor, lawyer, Indian chief."*

Matt scratched out "Indian chief" and replaced it with *"Native American* chief."

"Isn't that a nursery rhyme?" Ruthie asked, staring at the page.

When Matt failed to reply, Ruthie studied the paper again and nodded. "Yep!" she declared confidently. "It *is* a nursery rhyme. But I think you got it wrong."

Matt ran his hands through his hair again. Ruthie was really getting on his nerves.

He put down his pen. "I'm working on a career plan here."

"A *career* plan! Now that's the kind of talk I like to hear," the Reverend Eric Camden said, walking into the kitchen with a hopeful smile.

He was wearing a spotless white shirt and khaki pants. A sport jacket was folded neatly over his arm. But he was still tying his tie, and not having much luck.

"Hey, Dad," Matt mumbled.

"Career planning is a wonderful thing," Rev. Camden continued. "And welcome news to a father who's been sweating out tuition payments."

Matt closed his notepad with a snap.

"Deciding your major?" Rev. Camden asked.

Matt shot his dad a burning look.

"Try to see it my way, Matt," Rev. Camden said in his best fatherly tone. "Since it *is* the middle of the second semester and I haven't heard you mention anything about a major, I was just wondering if you'd made a decision yet. That's all."

Matt was rescued from this unwelcome discussion when his mother entered the kitchen. Annie Camden kissed her husband on the cheek and brushed a stray curl away from Ruthie's face.

Then she helped Rev. Camden put a proper Windsor knot in his tie.

"Your clients are in the living room, honey," Mrs. Camden said.

Matt raised his eyebrows. "Clients?"

Mrs. Camden put one hand on her hip. "They're people who come to your father for counseling. Just what would *you* call them?"

Matt rose, shrugged, and grabbed his black leather jacket from the coat rack.

"I don't know," he replied. "Mentally disturbed parishioners, maybe?"

His mother frowned.

"I got it!" Matt cried, pointing to his head. "Church nuts!"

Rev. Camden nodded patiently. "Just think about a major, Matt," he suggested.

"Got it, Dad," Matt said over his shoulder as he went out the back door to his car. He had a class at the university in an hour.

"You're going to have to choose a career someday!" Rev. Camden called after him. "Don't wait until you're forty!"

Matt started the car and gunned the engine, deliberately drowning out his father's voice. Then he backed out of the driveway.

"Whatever he does," Rev. Camden muttered, "I hope he doesn't major in psychology." He turned to Mrs. Camden. "So where are the church nuts?" he asked.

"They're in the den cooing over the twins." Mrs. Camden shook her head. "I just don't understand these babies," she said. "David and Samuel cried all night. But now that we have company, the two of them are acting like perfect angels!"

"You *always* think they're perfect angels!" Ruthie put in.

She jumped up and ran out of the room.

"Hey, what's the matter with you?" Mrs. Camden cried. But Ruthie was already gone.

"I'll, uh, take care of my...clients," Rev. Camden said. "And maybe you should take care of Ruthie. She seems to resent the attention the twins are getting."

Mrs. Camden nodded. "It's going to be

hard on Ruthie now. She's not the baby of the family anymore."

Just then, the babies' cries interrupted their conversation.

Rev. Camden took his wife's hand. "Join me in the den," he said. "You can take care of the twins. I'll take care of the church nuts."

"I can't believe you called me out of the blue like this," Mary said into the phone as she plopped on her bed.

"I hope it's okay," Wilson said.

"Hey, don't worry about it," Mary insisted. "Lucy and I have our own line now. We can talk all night if we want to."

"Well, I know it's a little early," Wilson said. "But I wanted to catch you before you went to school."

"It's okay, really!" Mary replied. She was thrilled to hear from her ex-boyfriend. "There's no such thing as early around here. Not since the twins were born."

"I know how *that* is," Wilson said sympathetically. He had a three-year-old son, Billy.

Just then, Lucy returned from the bathroom.

"I'm ready!" she announced.

Mary turned away from her sister. "I'm not alone right now," she said in a low voice to Wilson.

Lucy rolled her eyes in disgust.

"Let's go, Mary!" she whispered urgently. "We're going to be late!"

Mary covered the receiver. "Give me a little privacy," she hissed.

Lucy tossed her head and stalked out of the bedroom. Mary made a rude face at Lucy's back, then returned to her conversation.

"So you missed me, huh?" Mary teased.

"Yeah, I did, and I still *do*," Wilson replied. He sounded sincere.

"So to what trick of fate do I owe this unexpected call?" Mary asked.

Wilson laughed. "I've just been thinking about you, that's all." He paused.

"I guess I've been trying to get up the courage to call you for a couple of weeks now, Mary," he said softly.

"You *have?*" Mary replied, trying to sound casual. "Why? I won't bite your head off or anything."

"I know," Wilson answered. "It's just that I've been thinking about you, and us, and all the fun we used to have together."

Mary sighed wistfully. "I miss those

times, too." She could almost imagine his sweet smile. Mary realized that she'd missed Wilson more than she thought. Time away from him had healed the old wounds of their breakup. His unwillingness to commit to her and the discovery that he had a son by a previous girlfriend who had died were forgotten. Now Mary remembered only the good things about their relationship.

"So what has all your thinking led up to?" she asked.

"I guess I was thinking that we should maybe get together...like, tonight."

A thrill rushed through Mary.

"Well, that *does* sound nice," she said trying to stay cool. "What time?"

"Say, eight o'clock," Wilson replied. "At Eddie's."

Mary felt another rush of adrenaline. Eddie's was their special place. Wilson had remembered!

"I'll be there," Mary promised.

Lucy returned to the bedroom just in time to hear the tail end of the conversation.

Mary took the phone away from her ear and covered the receiver again.

"Don't you have school today?" she

asked pointedly.

"Yes. And so do *you!*" Lucy said. "Now let's get going."

Simon appeared in the doorway, wearing his school pack. He caught Mary's eye and pointed to his Red Lightning watch.

"Sorry, Wilson," Mary whispered into the phone. "I've got to go or we'll be late for school. But I'll definitely see you tonight." She hung up quickly.

Lucy glared at her sister. "We'll meet you in the car," she told Simon without turning around. Simon nodded and disappeared, leaving his sisters alone again.

"You know perfectly well that neither of us is going *anywhere* tonight," Lucy said. "We're trapped here in Camden Penitentiary, all because of those babies."

As if to punctuate Lucy's words, the two girls heard the all-too-familiar cries of the twins sounding from the den.

Mary grabbed her bag and threw it over her shoulder. Before Lucy could say anything more, Mary was pushing her through the bedroom door.

"We'll talk later. Let's get out of here," Mary said. She covered her ears. "*Now!* Before I lose my mind."

*   *   *

Simon had gone back to his room. He'd forgotten something while he was getting ready for school. He went to his desk, grabbed three large books, and tucked them into his book bag.

Lately, Simon's reading material had changed. He'd completely stopped reading comics, including the adventures of his favorite character, Red Lightning.

These days, he had been concentrating on nonfiction. Specifically, he'd been reading self-help books about raising children since his little brothers were born.

As he was zipping his bag shut, Ruthie entered the room. She saw the books Simon was slipping in with his textbooks. While she didn't understand all of the titles, she knew what the books were about: Taking care of babies.

"Not you, too!" she cried.

"Not me *what?*" Simon asked.

"Oh, nothing," Ruthie answered, crossing her arms and turning her back on him.

"Look, Ruthie," Simon said. He took his sister by the shoulders and turned her around again. "I've got to go to school now, so I'm putting you in charge."

"In charge of what?" Ruthie asked.

"You've got to take care of Happy today.

And Mom and Dad, too. Things are a little crazy around here."

"I'll say," Ruthie declared.

Simon nodded. "And don't forget—"

"I know! I know!" Ruthie cried angrily. "Don't forget to take care of the *twins*."

"Actually, what I was going to say was don't forget to clean up your room," Simon said. "Your dolls are lying naked all over the floor in there, and you haven't made your bed yet, either!"

"My dolls need new outfits," Ruthie argued. "And I didn't make my bed because I don't think I'll be sleeping there tonight."

"Very funny," Simon replied.

"Today is your lucky day, Simon," Ruthie said. "I'll wait for you to come home from school. We can dress the dolls together."

Simon made a face. "No way! I've got my hands full taking care of Mom and Dad. They're pretty much lost since the twins came home."

"The twins! The twins!" Ruthie cried in frustration, covering her face. Then she ran from Simon's room.

In the corner, Happy whimpered.

Simon sighed. "What do you think is wrong with Ruthie?" he asked the dog.

Happy just barked in reply and wagged her tail.

Matt was halfway to campus when he realized he'd been worrying about the wrong thing.

For the last few weeks, he had been contemplating his future.

He'd been worried about his major—or lack of one. He'd been worried about getting a degree and going to graduate school. He'd even considered joining the military. There was something romantic and exciting about a career as an officer and a gentleman. And the military paid for your education—or a lot of it, anyway. It wouldn't be so bad following in the footsteps of his grandfather, the Colonel.

But in the end, Matt hadn't signed up because he had been seized with doubt. Not just about the military, but about his future in general.

Matt didn't doubt that he could find a career eventually. What he did wonder was whether he was really *ready* to find one.

What's the point of a career, anyway? Matt asked himself. *Some people simply have* jobs. *They just work every day to make money.*

Matt sighed. He could sure use some money himself. But this whole problem had him tied up in knots.

Then, as he was waiting at a very long red light, Matt had a breakthrough. *I don't need to focus on a career right now,* he realized. *What I really need is a job. A simple, ordinary, paying job.*

And that is something I can find right now. Today.

Matt frowned as the light turned green and he hit the gas pedal. Where was he going to find a job?

Just then, he drove past the local strip mall. An eatery called the Dairy Shack—a popular hangout—was located at the far end of the line of shops and businesses. Cars surrounded the place, and people were heading inside for early morning coffee and doughnuts.

Then he saw it: The huge Dairy Shack sign looming over the parking lot, its message spelled out in plastic letters.

HELP WANTED, the sign read. MUST HAVE OWN CAR.

Matt checked his watch. "Forty-five minutes until class," he said out loud.

The decision, it seemed, had been made for him.

As Matt swerved the car into the parking lot, he almost laughed out loud. He couldn't wait to see the look on his father's face when he discovered that his oldest son finally had a job!

"See you after school," Simon told his sisters with a wave of his hand as he headed for class. But over his shoulder, he eyed the two of them suspiciously. Mary had gunned the engine and pulled away from the curb like a shot.

"Finally, we can talk!" Lucy declared.

Mary ignored her sister as she carefully steered the car through the crowded high school parking lot.

"Listen to me. You are *not* going out on a date tonight!" Lucy decreed.

"Why not? It's Friday."

"You're not going out on a date because *I* don't have a date."

"Oh, no," Mary said, with a shake of her head. "That is just not fair. Why should *I* have to suffer because *you're* a loser?"

Lucy shrugged off the insult. "If you go out tonight, I'll be the one stuck helping Mom and Dad with the twins."

"So? I'd do it for you."

Lucy eyed Mary skeptically. "Oh. Right. *Sure* you would."

"Come on, Lucy," Mary pleaded. "This is the first chance I've had to see Wilson since we broke up."

Lucy snorted.

"I just need to see how I feel about him now," Mary declared.

"No way." Lucy shook her head.

Mary pulled into a tight parking space and cut the engine.

"Please, Lucy," Mary said in a soft voice. "Don't make me beg."

Lucy looked out the car window.

"Wilson even asked me to meet him at Eddie's—do you know what that *means?*" Mary said.

Lucy nodded. "I guess."

She knew that things had never been the same between Mary and Wilson after what had happened at Eddie's several weeks ago. Mary had wanted Wilson to tell her that he loved her.

But Wilson wasn't ready to say that, and they'd had a major fight that night.

A silent moment passed. Finally, Lucy sighed and her expression softened.

Got her! Mary thought triumphantly.

"Okay," Lucy said, relenting. "You can go out tonight and I'll cover the twins. But only if Mom and Dad agree."

"Come on, Lucy! You know they'll never let me go! After spending all day with the twins, they want to use us both for slave labor."

"We should ask them anyway," Lucy insisted.

"Okay," Mary agreed. "Plan A, we ask their permission. Plan B, you cover for me for an hour or so while I sneak out."

"Oh, no, you don't!"

"*Please*, Lucy?" Mary said. "You've got to do it. For me. For Wilson. For both our futures…"

Her voice trailed off, but she continued to plead with her eyes.

Lucy sighed. *I know I'm going to get the wrong end of this stick,* she thought bitterly. But she finally agreed anyway.

"Oh, thank you! Thank you!" Mary squealed, hugging her sister in gratitude.

"But I don't have to like it," Lucy muttered to herself, and opened the car door.

Even though he'd been to the Dairy Shack a million times, Matt felt a tingle of apprehension the moment he pushed through the glass doors. He'd just realized at that moment that he was about to have an actual job interview.

He quickly ran his hand through his hair in an attempt to make himself look more presentable. Then he adjusted his broad shoulders inside his leather jacket, took a deep breath, and stepped up to the counter.

The place was pretty empty now. Only two couples in the booths and no one in the takeout line.

It must be that downtime between the breakfast and lunch rushes, Matt figured. It was the same at the university cafeteria during this time of day.

"Can I help you?" a voice asked.

Matt turned and came face-to-face with a very attractive young woman in a waitress uniform. She was almost as tall as he was, with long blond hair pulled up under the silly paper cap all Dairy Shack employees sported.

Matt figured she wasn't much older than he was. And she was pretty enough to make the paper hat look kind of cute.

She smiled at him. "Would you like to take a seat?" she asked.

"Uh, no," Matt stammered. "But you

can help me."

He paused to get himself together. *I'm not exactly making a great first impression,* he thought glumly.

"I...I wonder if I could speak to the manager?" he asked finally.

"Sure!" the woman replied. "You're talking to her. I'm Terri, Terri Fadden."

"Matt...Matt Camden."

As they shook hands, Terri studied him carefully.

"College guy?" she asked.

Matt nodded. "Yeah. City. Second semester."

Terri nodded. "I went there for two years, but I had to drop out." She sighed sadly. "So, what can I do for you?"

"Well, I saw the sign, and—"

"And you're looking for a job," Terri interrupted.

Matt nodded. Terri looked unimpressed. "I have my own car," Matt said quickly.

"How is your driving record?" she asked.

"Perfect," Matt answered. "No accidents. No tickets."

"We only have two openings, both for the night shift," Terri warned him.

"I have class in the daytime," Matt replied. "Night shift would be better for me, if it's good for you."

Terri nodded. "I guess this could work."

A customer rose from one of the booths and Terri rang up his bill.

"The delivery job pays minimum wage, plus tips," she told him. "Sometimes the tips are good. Sometimes they're not so good."

Matt nodded.

"But working delivery instead of in the kitchen has some perks," Terri added with a smile.

"Like what?" Matt asked.

"Well, for one thing, you don't have to wear a Dairy Shack uniform. Or the hat."

"Well, that's a relief," Matt confessed.

Terri opened a drawer under the cash register and pulled out an official-looking form. Then she gave him a pen and the blank job application.

"Fill that out while I pour you some coffee."

"Thanks," Matt said. When he was done filling out the application, Terri asked him about his school schedule and how many hours he thought he could work each week. She seemed satisfied with his answers.

Finally, Matt rose. "Well, I've got to get to class," he announced. "Thanks for the coffee."

"Nice to meet you, Matt," Terri said.

"So, is somebody going to call me and let me know if I got the job?" Matt asked finally.

Terri laughed. "Welcome to Dairy Shack," she said, handing him an introductory brochure. "Read this pamphlet and report for work tonight at seven-thirty."

"Great!" Matt cried. "Thanks a lot!"

"That's seven-thirty, *sharp!*"

"Can't wait," Matt said as he waved good-bye.

What a great boss! he thought as he walked back to the car. *This work thing might actually be fun.*

Matt savored his incredible luck for the rest of the drive to campus.

How many guys have an easy job, and a very pretty boss? he wondered. He couldn't wait to start work!

TWO

As Rev. Camden climbed the stairs to his bedroom, he could hear the twins crying.

Tired, he thought. *I'm so tired.*

In the days since David and Sam had arrived, neither he nor his wife had gotten an uninterrupted night's sleep. The constant feedings, changings, and cranky crying had taken a toll on them both.

It won't go on like this forever, he reminded himself. *We've gone through this before. Five times.*

A loud wail greeted him.

"You're just in time," his wife said. "They *both* need changing."

"Sure, honey," Rev. Camden replied. "Just let me hang up my jacket and tie."

"Hurry," Mrs. Camden said.

Draping the sport jacket over the back of a chair, Rev. Camden took up position over Samuel's crib. His wife passed behind him, clutching David in her arms. She handed her husband a clean diaper, which he threw over his shoulder.

"Hello, Sam!"

Rev. Camden leaned over the crib and greeted his son with a wide grin. "I'm here to fix everything," he said as he fumbled with the diaper.

But just as Rev. Camden got the diaper open, Samuel opened fire.

A yellow fountain rose into the air, splashing on Rev. Camden's white shirt.

Rev. Camden gasped in surprise and pulled away. "I can't believe that happened," he cried in exasperation. "Again!"

"That wasn't very nice," Mrs. Camden told Samuel. "Daddy is very tired."

In the other crib, David's cries became louder and more insistent.

Rev. and Mrs. Camden exchanged harried glances. Their new bundles of joy were even more of a handful than they'd anticipated.

The twins' cries were the first sound to greet Matt's ears as he entered the house.

The screen door slammed shut behind him.

"Oh, no," he said. "Not again."

Upstairs, Rev. and Mrs. Camden looked at each other hopefully.

"Was that the back door?" Mrs. Camden asked.

Rev. Camden nodded excitedly. "I think so," he replied.

Creeping toward the bedroom door, he slowly, quietly reached for the doorknob.

"Stay calm," he told his wife. "We don't want to alert our prey, or they'll flee."

In the downstairs foyer, Mary, Lucy, Simon, and Ruthie had just entered the house.

Mary and Lucy were still discussing their chances of going out that night. They were careful not to mention Mary's planned escape if all did not go well.

"I'm telling you, the kid eats other people's lunches," Ruthie was telling Simon. "Even worse, he smells like your shoes!"

Simon shot his sister a sour glance. "If you don't like how my shoes smell, don't *sniff* them."

"This isn't about your shoes," Ruthie replied. "It's about this kid I sit next to in class. *And* on the bus. He smells."

Simon nodded. "Here's the solution. It's simple. Fake like you can't see the blackboard and the teacher will move you closer to the front," he said.

"But how do I do that?" she asked.

"Squint," Simon said, demonstrating.

"Okay," Ruthie said.

Matt rushed out of the kitchen. "Ssshhhh! Quiet!" he demanded in a harsh whisper.

They all stared at him.

"Do you want Mom and Dad to hear you?" Matt hissed.

Understanding dawned on everyone's faces. They could hear the echoing cries of the twins coming from the top of the stairs. Matt pointed toward the ceiling.

"They're waiting for us," he whispered ominously. "You know they are."

Ruthie covered her ears.

"They're waiting for someone to help them stop that crying," Matt continued.

Lucy sighed. "We're trapped," she said.

"Listen," Mary said. "I've figured all the angles. I think we can use the noise to our advantage."

Matt shot her a questioning glance.

"We can use their crying for *cover*,"

Mary explained. "If we sneak into our rooms very, *very* quietly, Mom and Dad won't be able to hear us over all the screaming." She smiled smugly.

"Sounds like a plan," Matt said.

On a silent three-count from Mary, all five kids tiptoed up the steps.

Rev. and Mrs. Camden were waiting for them.

"At last," Rev. Camden said. "Reinforcements."

"They've got a plan," Mrs. Camden said.

"But we're smarter," the reverend said quickly.

"This is their first weekend with all seven children here," his wife whispered. "And as helpful as they might seem, they're going to try to take advantage of the situation. You do know that, don't you?"

Rev. Camden grinned. "Sure, but I love a challenge."

They both leaned against the bedroom door, waiting to spring their trap.

Matt took the lead as the Camden kids moved up the stairs in combat formation.

Things went great until Mary hit the

sixth step. The *squeaky* step.

They all froze. But the only sound they heard was the wails of the babies.

When Matt reached the top of the steps, he moved aside and waved the rest of them past.

Just then, Rev. and Mrs. Camden stepped into the hall, the twins bawling in their arms. The kids froze again.

"Look honey," their father said in mock surprise. "The children are home!"

"*All* of them," Mrs. Camden added.

Two hours later, Mary and Lucy were upstairs, cowering in their room. They'd both used homework as an excuse to isolate themselves from the rest of the family.

Mrs. Camden had reminded the girls that it was Friday.

"I want to get an early start," Lucy said. "I have to write five pages on the Constitution."

"And I have a psych exam," Mary insisted.

Mrs. Camden let them off the hook— for now.

Simon, meanwhile, was holed up in his room. He *was* hard at work. At least, that's the way *he* saw it.

Simon had just finished reading a book called *Raising Boys Right*. Now he was starting another thick volume. It was called *Twins: The Terror and the Joy*.

Matt was the only one not to offer an excuse. He was taking a shower.

Ruthie was in her parents' room with her mom. She lay sprawled on the edge of the bed, quietly singing. Mrs. Camden sat next to her, lulled by her youngest daughter's soft voice.

Mercifully, both twins were sound asleep. They snuggled warmly in their mother's arms.

"Sometimes I feel like a motherless child... a long, long way from home..." Ruthie crooned, her voice wistful.

She glanced over her shoulder to make sure her mother was listening.

Their eyes met.

"Ruthie, you are not a motherless child," Mrs. Camden said. "Your mother is right here. I know you want my attention, but I am a little busy right now."

Just as Ruthie was about to answer, David gurgled and began to stir.

"I could use your help, you know," Mrs. Camden told Ruthie as she shifted David in her arm. "You're a big sister now, so you're more important than ever."

Ruthie frowned. "All right, all right," she said. "What do you want me to do?"

"How about if you hold Sam while I feed David?" Mrs. Camden asked.

"I don't want to see you feed either one of them again until they're eating with knives and forks," Ruthie said. She jumped off the bed and bolted out of the room.

"Ruthie, wait!" her mother cried, instantly waking Sam.

In the hall, Ruthie paused. But as soon as she heard her mom cooing to the babies, she walked away.

"How does this look?" Mary asked Lucy as she twirled around. She wore her favorite black pants and a white ribbed sweater.

Lucy shrugged. "What do you care, Miss I-don't-have-to-dress-to-impress-boys?"

Mary smiled. "You're jealous."

"Well, duh," Lucy retorted.

Lucy attempted to study while Mary tried on different outfits. The clothes ended up in a heap on her bed.

"Can I ask you an honest question?" Lucy said suddenly.

"Sure, shoot."

"Why *do* you care how you look? You and Wilson aren't seeing each other anymore."

Mary thought about that for a moment. "He won," she said finally. "I lost. I wanted him to like me and he didn't."

"So what?" Lucy replied. "Love isn't some kind of hoops game. Is that what tonight's all about? Mary vs. Wilson, the rematch?"

"No," Mary said as she squinted into the mirror. "But I don't like to lose. At anything. So I'm going to ambush him."

She dabbed on a bit of Lucy's lipstick. "I want to look good tonight," she continued. "Just to show Wilson what he's been missing all these weeks."

Lucy frowned. She didn't want to argue, though. So she decided to change the subject. She pointed at the stack of clothes on Mary's bed.

"I think you'd better hang that stuff up fast. Either Mom, or Dad, or *both* of them are going to barge in here any second now.

"You don't want them to figure out you're planning to escape from Camden Penitentiary, do you?"

*   *   *

Downstairs in his study, Rev. Camden heard the shower stop. *That means the bathroom's free,* he thought. *I'd better be quick.* He leaped to his feet.

Mine! Rev. Camden thought happily, pumping his fist. *The shower is mine!*

He was already up the stairs and halfway down the hall when he collided with Matt.

Rev. Camden raised his eyebrows.

Matt was wearing his black leather jacket. His hair was neatly combed, and he clutched his car keys in his right hand.

"Where are you going?" Rev. Camden demanded.

Matt smiled. His father had instantly deduced something was up.

"You'd better come up with something pretty important, because we're counting on *all* of you kids for some help with the twins tonight," Rev. Camden said.

Matt crossed his arms and nodded.

"I *am* going somewhere important," he announced. "I'm going to the Dairy Shack."

Rev. Camden blinked.

"Dad, I got a job!" Matt cried. "They started a new delivery service. I'm one of the first drivers they hired."

Rev. Camden nodded. "I see. Your car...or their car?"

Matt stared at the floor. "My car," he muttered.

"So how much does it pay?"

"Minimum wage, plus tips."

"Hmm," his father said. "What about mileage?"

"Mileage?"

"You know," Rev. Camden prompted. "Gas money? Money for wear and tear on your car? Insurance?"

"No," Matt confessed, "nothing like that. But it pays tuition."

Rev. Camden was taken aback. "Tuition?" he said. "Really?"

Matt nodded. "The woman who hired me gave me a brochure." He pulled the folder out of his jacket pocket and showed it to his father.

"It says right here that, if you work there twenty hours a week and go to college full-time, they pay one-fourth of your tuition for the fourth year."

Rev. Camden smiled skeptically. "You think this job is going to last three years?"

"Well," Matt said, "it *could*. I mean, it's just driving around. How hard is that?"

Rev. Camden nodded again. "I'll bet

you fifty bucks that your job doesn't last the night."

Now it was Matt's turn to be taken aback.

"Why would you bet against me?" Matt demanded. "I mean, you're my *dad*."

Rev. Camden held up his hand. "Because, one," he said, raising a finger, "you have yet to realize what any job is really about.

"And two," he continued, counting off, "I need the fifty bucks. I've got two more mouths to feed."

Matt smiled at his father. "Make it twenty and you're on!"

Rev. Camden found his wife in their room, feeding the twins. The newspaper was spread out on the bed in front of her.

"There's a sale on diapers at Baby-world," she informed him.

"I'll go there tomorrow," Rev. Camden said, rubbing his hands together. "I feel twenty bucks richer already."

"What?" his wife asked.

"Oh, nothing." He pointed in the general direction of the kitchen. "Shall I go start dinner?"

Mrs. Camden shook her head. "Mary

and Lucy can handle that," she told him. "You should try to grab a fifteen-minute nap."

"Sounds like a plan," Rev. Camden said.

"But first, please put Simon on permanent Ruthie duty until further notice," his wife added.

"I'm on my way." Rev. Camden said, with a wave of his hand.

Simon sat at his desk. He'd finished skimming *Twins: The Terror and the Joy* and had just picked up *So...Now You're a Dad*.

A whimper from Happy interrupted Simon's concentration. He looked up from his book. Happy was sitting next to his chair, a leash in her mouth.

"I'll be right with you, girl," he promised.

There was a knock, and Rev. Camden came in. He blinked when he saw Simon's book.

"Shouldn't you be reading *So...Now You're a Big Brother?*" he asked.

Simon ignored his father's gibe.

Just then, a baby began to cry in the next room. Simon shook his head. "Dad, you've got to get those kids on a schedule."

Rev. Camden stared at Simon. *Do I really have the time and energy to straighten him out now?* he wondered. *No way.*

"Simon," Rev. Camden said patiently, "while I appreciate your advice, your mother and I think we know what we're doing at this point. We *have* done this a few times already, you know."

Simon snapped the book shut. "Oh, really?" he said smugly. "Cause it's been seven—almost *eight*—years since you two have had an infant around this place. Parenting isn't what it used to be."

He stared at his father. "Have you been keeping up with all the new techniques?"

Rev. Camden came up blank. "Uh, well…"

"I didn't think so."

Maybe this is *the right time to straighten Simon out,* Rev. Camden decided. Then he got ahold of himself. *Patience is a virtue,* he reminded himself.

"Look, son," he said, a smile plastered on his face. "If I spend a lot of time talking to you, I'm not going to get a nap. Do you know what you can do to make things easier?"

Simon shrugged. "No. What?"

"Find Ruthie, welcome her into the

wonderful world of being an older sibling, and show her how it's done. I think she's having a problem adjusting right now. Okay? Thanks."

He went out the door but stuck his head back in a moment later.

"And walk the dog," he added, pointing at Happy. The dog whimpered gratefully.

"Sure, Dad," Simon said, and returned to his book.

Rev. Camden rushed downstairs to the den, where a soft couch was waiting for him. He gently closed the glass double doors and sat down. He sighed as he settled into the soft cushions.

But his head had barely touched the pillow when he remembered one last thing he had to do. He rose reluctantly and ran back up the steps.

Mary had barely finished hanging up all her rejected outfits when there was a knock at the door. She and Lucy exchanged worried glances.

Rev. Camden poked his head through the door.

"Start dinner, please," he commanded.

From her bed, Lucy snapped her textbook shut and rolled her eyes. "What do you want us to cook?"

"It doesn't matter," he replied.

"But—" Mary began.

"Look," Rev. Camden continued, "I don't have time to talk. I'm already wasting my meager nap time."

Mary nudged Lucy. "Uh, Dad," Lucy said quickly. "If we cook dinner, could we go out later? Run some errands? Anything?"

"No!" Rev. Camden said, with a shake of his head. "No one can go out. No one is going anywhere until your mother and I get eight hours of sleep."

He fixed his gaze on his daughters. "That's eight *consecutive* hours. Not total. Is that understood?"

Lucy sighed. "I was just asking,"

"Well, don't," Rev. Camden told her.

Almost immediately, he realized he'd been too harsh. "I'm sorry," he apologized. "I'm just over-tired and overwhelmed."

"Eric!" his wife called.

He smiled weakly at Lucy and Mary. Then he ran to the bedroom and peeked in.

"I need a towel," Mrs. Camden said.

Rev. Camden turned toward the bathroom—then realized Matt had used the last clean towel for his shower. He remembered that there were more towels in the dryer—downstairs. Rev. Camden bolted toward the steps.

Mary turned to Lucy.

"Don't say it," Lucy begged.

"Sorry," Mary said. "We have to go to Plan B."

_____

THREE

Lucy pounded the bed with her fists. "No! No! Not Plan B!"

"I'm afraid so," Mary said. "And I can't do it myself. I need you, Lucy…"

Lucy groaned.

"Mom and Dad won't let me leave the house," Mary went on. "At best, they'll tell Wilson to come over here.

"Bringing a date here is just wrong, and you know it," Mary continued. "*No one should have to be here!*"

Lucy was still torn by doubt.

"What if things were reversed?" Mary pressed. "How would you like to have *your* date come over here, and both of you have to listen to those babies crying. And—"

"I get it! I get it!" Lucy cried, covering her ears.

"So you understand where I'm coming from," Mary said quietly.

Lucy nodded. "Okay. I'll do it."

Mary threw her arms around her sister. "You're the best!" she cried.

"I'll cover for you, but not for very long," Lucy warned. "Mom and Dad are so busy they probably won't even miss you for an hour or so...I hope."

Mary hugged her sister again. Then she looked at the clock.

"It's almost five-thirty!" she cried.

"Well, act casual," Lucy cautioned. "They'll be watching us at dinner."

Rev. Camden arrived at his bedroom door with an armload of towels. Ruthie was sitting in one of the twins' cribs.

"Where's your mother?" he asked, pretending not to notice anything strange.

Ruthie shrugged. "Who do you mean?" she asked. "I have no mother."

"Ruthie—" Rev. Camden began. Then he stopped himself. *Annie can handle this better than I can,* he decided.

"You know," he continued, "you used to fit into one of those."

"I still fit," Ruthie insisted.

"You know what would be great?" Rev. Camden said. But Ruthie shook her head even before he'd finished his thought.

"If it's a great way to help you with the babies, forget it!" Ruthie said stubbornly.

"Okay," Rev. Camden replied. Then he put his arms around his daughter.

"Come on," he insisted. "You're going to have to get out of this cradle before it breaks and you hurt yourself."

Ruthie began to squirm. "I don't want to get out!" she cried.

"Well, you have to," Rev. Camden said, more sternly. "Come on, let's go!"

Ruthie squealed in outrage.

"Mom-meeeee!"

Having finally decided on a casual striped sweater and jeans, Mary was practically on her way to meet Wilson. All she had to do was get through dinner without her parents suspecting anything—and she was out of there. Right now, she and Lucy were heading for the kitchen.

The girls were on the stairs when Ruthie's scream echoed off the walls.

"Hurry!" Mary whispered to Lucy, pushing her forward.

Unfortunately, they didn't get past the living room.

"Hey!" Mrs. Camden cried, still clutching both twins in her arms. "I could use a little help here."

The girls crossed the foyer. Mary gathered David into her arms. Lucy took Samuel. Both twins instantly began to cry.

"I'll be right back," Mrs. Camden promised as she bolted up the stairs.

Lucy and Mary looked at the babies in their arms. Then they looked at each other.

"The crying," Mary muttered. "I can't take it anymore."

Mrs. Camden's eyes widened in surprise at the scene that greeted her in her bedroom.

"Daddy hurt me!" Ruthie cried.

Rev. Camden stepped away from his daughter, stung by Ruthie's accusation.

"Come here, honey," Mrs. Camden cooed, taking Ruthie in her arms. "Where does it hurt?"

Ruthie thought for a minute. "My foot," she decided.

Rev. Camden looked at his wife. "I didn't touch her foot."

"Come with me," Mrs. Camden said, still cradling Ruthie. "I'll clean you up and we'll put a boo-boo strip on your foot."

"Okay," Ruthie sniffled.

As Mrs. Camden stepped past her husband, Ruthie shot him an "I won" look.

"After we fix your boo-boo," Mrs. Camden said. "Mommy is going to take a nap."

Rev. Camden looked at his watch hopefully. His time was up. He'd lost his chance. "So close," he sighed.

He stood there for a moment, rubbing his tired eyes. Then he heard a pathetic whimper at his feet.

Happy stared up at him with her big black eyes. The leash was still in her mouth.

Rev. Camden strode angrily across the hall toward Simon's room.

"Ka-BOOM!" Billy screamed.

Wilson, who was struggling to put a clean shirt on his son, grabbed at the toddler. But Billy squirmed out of Wilson's arms and scooted to the other end of the room, quick as lightning.

"Come on, Billy," Wilson pleaded. "The baby-sitter will be here soon."

Billy squealed. "Debbie's coming!"

"Right. And you've got to get ready."

Usually, Wilson enjoyed his son's antics. But not tonight. He was tired from work. Even worse, he'd just paid out most of what he'd earned to the daytime baby-sitter.

Now he'd have to come up with more cash for Debbie, the night sitter. His aunt watched Billy most days. But she was out of town.

"Let's go, Billy," Wilson said sternly.

Billy ignored his father.

"Remember my promise," Wilson said finally.

Billy climbed onto the sagging, thread-bare couch and jumped up and down.

"I get chocolots-a-milk when Debbie comes!" Billy cried.

"But only if you're *good*," Wilson reminded him. "Now get down from there before you get hurt."

"Chocolots-a-milk!" Billy squawked, throwing up his arms. The sudden motion caused him to lose his balance. He crashed to the floor.

Sprawled on the rug, Billy blinked in shock. Then he began to wail.

"Are you okay?" Wilson cried.

Heart racing with panic, he quickly checked his son's arms and legs for bruises or broken bones. But the child seemed more surprised than hurt.

Wilson held Billy close.

The little boy was still crying when the phone rang.

Lucy squinted to make out the directions on the Tuna Helper box. Her eyes were filled with painful onion tears, making reading difficult.

"So what do you think Wilson wants to talk to me about?" Mary asked.

"Maybe he just needs a friend," Lucy said.

"A *friend?*" Mary was incredulous. "That's the last thing I need."

"Maybe he's lonely," Jucy said.

"Wilson has a son, Lucy," Mary said. "A child who lives with him all the time. And he's got his aunt. And he works. He probably has friends at work, too."

"Sure," Lucy agreed. "Maybe he even has a girlfriend at work."

Mary frowned. "He sounded friendly... even normal, for Wilson," she said. "But I had this feeling there was something..."

"Well, you'll find out in a few hours," Lucy said. She pointed to the bubbling skillet on the stove. "It's time for you to help me make Tuna Helper."

"What should I do?" asked Mary.

"Well, it says here you can use celery and peppers for added zest," Lucy replied. "Look around and see if we have any."

Mary buried her head in the refrigerator. "I found celery!" she announced. "Red peppers, too!"

"Now cut them into teeny-tiny pieces, okay?" Lucy said.

Mary saluted. "Aye, aye, captain!"

A few minutes later, Lucy dumped the freshly cut vegetables into the skillet. They began to sizzle. Then she added the Tuna Helper ingredients, and water, and stirred.

Lucy read the directions again. "All it has to do is simmer for fifteen minutes," she announced.

"Good. I'll set the table," Mary said.

Lucy began to make a salad. Then she put some bread and butter on the table. But as she stirred the Tuna Helper, Lucy couldn't help thinking that she'd forgotten something...

I can't believed my baby-sitter bailed, Wilson thought bitterly. *What am I supposed to do now?*

He was supposed to meet Mary in less

than an hour. He glanced at Billy. The boy
was having fun, drinking milk and coloring
wild patterns on a piece of paper with his
crayons.

Wilson grabbed his address book.

*There has to be someone I can call to
take care of Billy for a few hours,* he
thought. *There just has to be.*

Wilson began to dial the first baby-
sitter on the list. He considered calling
Mary and warning her that he might be a
little late. But he dismissed that idea immediately.

She'd just use it as an excuse to bail, too,
he decided. And he really needed to see her
in person.

When no one answered the phone,
Wilson hung up and found another number. He got an answering machine.

Come on, come on, he thought as he
flipped through the pages of his tattered
address book.

There's got to be someone who will help.

Wilson glanced at his son. He loved
Billy more than anything, but sometimes
he couldn't help feeling sorry for himself.

*All I need is a couple of hours to do
what I want for a change...just a couple of
hours.*

*   *   *

"Here's the last of them," Simon announced, dumping a pile of dirty dishes into the soapy water.

"Hey! Watch it!" Mary cried, ducking the splash.

"Sorry," said Simon. He turned to Lucy. "What was that stuff, anyway?"

"Tuna Helper," Lucy replied.

"So there was supposed to be *tuna* in it, right?"

Lucy looked at Mary. Mary pointed at two unopened cans of tuna on the counter.

"He's right," Mary said. "It was just the Helper."

She picked the empty Tuna Helper box out of the trash and read the instructions.

"Yep," she concluded. "We were supposed to add the tuna."

"Ohhhhh." Lucy looked stricken.

"Maybe I'll call the Dairy Shack and get a delivery," Simon suggested.

Mary shrugged. "I'm fine with just the Helper."

"Me, too," Lucy added. "It was quite zesty."

"Well, *I'm* not!" Simon pulled the Dairy Shack menu off the refrigerator magnet and left the kitchen. Mary and Lucy were alone at last.

"Okay, okay!" Mary cried, glancing at the clock. "I've got to go."

Lucy paled.

Mary seized her sister's shoulders.

"Look," she said. "Don't lose your nerve now. I'll be back in an hour. I promise. If anyone is looking for me, just act like I just left the room or something."

Lucy stared back at her with disbelief. "You call that a *plan?*"

"Yes," Mary nodded. "Plan B. Remember?"

"So what do I do?"

"When someone says, 'Where's Mary?' you say, 'Gee, you just missed her.' Got it?"

Lucy shook her head. "You should really stay at home a while longer and work on a better plan."

"Too late," Mary said, grabbing her purse and jacket. "Gotta go. Wish me luck."

"Good luck," Lucy said. She had a sick feeling in the pit of her stomach.

But as Mary slipped out the door, Lucy felt certain that it was she—not her sister— who would be needing luck tonight.

Mary's heart was racing as she crossed the

darkened driveway. She stayed in the shadows until she reached the car. Glancing around, she carefully opened the door.

She looked back toward the house as she climbed behind the wheel. Her parents' window overlooked the driveway. Luckily, the curtains were drawn.

Mary started the car, praying that the noise would not be heard inside the house. Just to be safe, she kept the headlights off until she pulled out onto the street.

She didn't breathe again until she had turned the corner.

As she drove, tried to imagine what might happen during her evening with Wilson. Was he going to tell her that he wanted her back? Was he finally going to tell her he loved him? Or did he just want to be friends?

There's only one way to find out, Mary thought.

Rev. Camden quickly closed the curtain so Mary wouldn't see him spying on her.

"She's backing out of the driveway," he announced, giving his wife a conspiratorial grin.

Mrs. Camden sighed. "I'm not surprised," she said.

"You're not?" Rev. Camden said.

"Nope," Mrs. Camden replied. "I *knew* she was up to something. Did you see the way she was dressed at dinner?"

"Actually, no," Rev. Camden confessed. "I was too busy searching for the tuna in my casserole."

When his wife failed to laugh, Rev. Camden's tone suddenly turned serious. "So what do you think that 'something' is?" he asked.

They looked at each other and nodded. "A guy," they said in unison.

Matt pulled into the strip mall parking lot. It was almost seven, and in the autumn darkness, the lot was pretty empty—except around the brightly lit Dairy Shack. He slid his car into one of the spots marked DAIRY SHACK PERSONNEL ONLY.

He cut the engine and pocketed the keys. Then he pulled a comb from his pocket and ran it through his hair.

"Ready to see the boss again," Matt decided after he checked himself in the rear view mirror. He climbed out of the car, straightened his jacket, and approached the employee entrance.

*   *   *

Wilson turned off the water and stared into the bathroom mirror, listening for his son.

That's funny, he thought. *I was sure I heard Billy's voice talking to someone.*

Grabbing the cleanest towel he could find, Wilson wiped his face and opened the bathroom door.

"Billy?" he called. His voice sounded extra loud in the tiny apartment.

He heard a giggle. Then he heard a woman's voice.

Wilson bolted for the living room.

Billy was sitting in the middle of the floor with the telephone in his lap. He held the receiver to his ear.

"Hold on now, I can hear you breathing," the woman on the phone said, with growing agitation. "I'll call the phone company."

Wilson grabbed the phone away from his son. "Sorry," he told the worried woman, and hung up

"Billy, what were you doing?" Wilson demanded.

"Calling Debbie, the baby-watcher," Billy replied, pouting. "I want Debbie to read me a story."

"I'll read you a story, cowboy," Wilson said, picking him up. "But later. Okay?"

Billy nodded.

"I hope you dialed a local call, at least," Wilson muttered under his breath. "Come on, Billy," he said, sighing. "Do you want to go for a ride?"

Billy yawned and nodded. "Okay," he said.

Luckily, Billy was pretty cooperative as Wilson got him ready. He even perked up a bit when Wilson said they were going to see Mary Camden. Billy had always liked Mary.

Wilson looked at his watch. He was getting a late start.

I didn't want tonight to be like this, he thought bitterly. *And now I'm going to show up late.*

He searched the bedroom for his keys and finally located them in the pocket of the pants he'd worn to work that morning.

Wilson gave himself a last check in the mirror. He wore black jeans and a sleeveless black shirt that showed off the muscles in his arms.

I guess I look okay, he decided.

"Let's go, Billy!" Wilson called over his shoulder as he exited the bedroom.

But Billy was nowhere to be seen.

Then Wilson heard his son's giggle. It

was coming from the tiny kitchenette. Wilson raced across the apartment.

"Oh, no!" he cried.

Billy looked up at his father and grinned innocently.

He was sitting in the middle of the linoleum floor, a plastic cup by his side. A bit of milk—and a lot of chocolate sauce—were dripping down the sides of the cup.

Most of the rest of the sticky mess was all over the kitchen floor. And all over Billy.

FOUR

The odor of frying grease greeted Matt as he stepped into the Dairy Shack kitchen. Three of the goofiest-looking guys he'd ever seen were standing around an open stove. All of them wore Dairy Shack uniforms—complete with paper hats. One of them held a burning match.

It was obvious they were trying to relight the pilot inside the gas stove. But when Matt entered the area, the three looked up. One guy had wild red hair sticking out of his hat like a scouring pad. The second guy was crouched down, peering into the oven.

The third member of the trio could only be politely described as husky. He stared so intently at Matt that he forgot the hot match in his hand. He howled in surprise as the flame brushed his fingers.

"Ouch!" he yelped, dropping the burning ember on the hat of the guy looking into the oven. Instantly, the paper hat ignited.

The kid jumped up, pulled off the flaming hat, and threw it on the floor.

All three employees stamped on the smoldering headgear.

"I can't believe it," Matt told himself in awe. "It's the Three Stooges."

"Can I help you?" a rude, high-pitched voice demanded from behind him.

Matt whirled around, to face an arrogant-looking kid with a smug look on his buck-toothed face. He was shorter than Matt and wore a crisp white shirt—complete with a bow tie. The name ROGER DENBRO was emblazoned on a cheap plastic badge.

"This kitchen is for employees of the Dairy Shack only," Roger said.

Matt smiled. "And that would be *me*," he explained. "Could you run along and get the manager?"

The teenager glared at Matt. "You're *looking* at the manager!"

"You can't be," Matt said. "I mean...it

was a girl, umh…a *woman* who hired me. Her name was Terri. Terri Fadden!"

"Oh, so you're one of Terri's boys," Roger said.

"Yeah, I guess so," Matt replied.

"Well, Terri is the *day* manager," Roger said smugly. "My name is Roger Denbro, and I'm the *night* manager."

Matt frowned. *I should quit right now,* he thought. Then he remembered the twenty-dollar bet he'd made with his father.

Matt swallowed his pride. He'd have to tough it out—at least for tonight.

"So just who might *you* be?" Roger demanded.

Matt smiled, getting his teeth. "I'm the new delivery guy," he replied. "My name's Matt. Matt Camden."

He stuck out his hand.

Roger recoiled from it as if Matt's hand were a squashed bug.

"We don't start deliveries for another hour," Roger informed him with a nasty grin. "But I'm quite sure we can put you to work in the meantime."

He turned, his beady eyes scanning the kitchen. Then his gaze rested on a pile of dirty dishes stacked up in the sink.

"I think a little training session is in

order," Roger announced. He pointed to the mess. "You can start with those."

Matt frowned.

"And there *will* be an inspection," Roger added.

The Three Stooges snickered at Matt from behind their boss.

Matt swallowed his pride and went over to the sink. *It's going to be a long, long night,* he thought.

"And oh, yes!" Roger added, with finger raised. "Finish that assignment quickly. Our nightly managerial lecture is mandatory."

"Lecture?" Matt said, puzzled.

"Yes," Roger replied. "I find these talks are good for discipline."

Roger went into the office and closed the door behind him. The Three Stooges went back to work, trying to light the oven. Matt was left alone with the dirty dishes.

He sighed. Then he hung up his jacket and rolled up his sleeves.

Mary arrived at Eddie's a little early, but the place was already packed.

Eddie's was a pool hall and coffeehouse, a popular place for kids to hang out on weekends.

At the entrance, Mary was nearly bowled over as two huge guys slammed through the glass double doors.

"Sorry!" Mary said, leaping back.

The taller of the two guys stopped dead in his tracks.

"Hey, it's our fault," he said. "Sorry. I hope we didn't hurt you."

Mary shook her head and smiled. "Hey, I can dodge anybody as big and slow as you two!"

"Oh, yeah?" the guy replied, smiling back. He had short dark hair, a deep dimple on his chin, and sparkling green eyes. And he was a good head taller than Mary.

The guy hesitated. He seemed to recognize her. He looked familiar to Mary, too.

"Do you, uh, go to Centerville?" he asked.

Mary shook her head, then blinked. She'd suddenly remembered who he was.

"Tommy Tryon, right?" she asked. "I watched you play Reed last week."

"We lost," Tommy said with a frown.

"I know," Mary replied. "But you threw a heck of a pass in the third quarter!"

To her surprise, Tommy Tryon blushed.

"I...I guess you go to Walter Reed, then," he stammered.

"Yep." Mary nodded.

"Hey, Tom," his friend called from the parking lot. "We gotta split, man."

"Oh, yeah...right." Tommy looked back at Mary. "Hey, I'm really sorry for almost blocking you just now. I, um, I hope we run into each other again—but not literally."

Mary laughed. "Well, I come to Eddie's a lot," she fibbed.

Tommy smiled, and Mary felt her knees grow weak. *He is* so *cute,* she thought.

"I'll look for you," Tommy said over his shoulder as he ran after his friend. "Hey wait," he called, stopping suddenly. "I don't know your name."

"Mary Camden."

"Nice to meet you, Mary Camden!"

Mary waved as Tommy hopped into a BMW and sped off.

Well, she thought, *that was cool.*

Getting herself together, Mary entered the pool hall.

As she was moving through the crowd, Mary couldn't help but notice that she turned more than a few male heads. And, some of the guys who were checking her out actually *knew* her! They saw her every day at school.

Tonight all of them seemed to be looking at her as if she were...well, some kind of *babe* or something.

It was weird. Exciting, but definitely weird.

I could get used to this, Mary decided.

The "managerial lecture" was just as painful as Matt had anticipated.

The first humiliation came when Matt was forced to line up, military-style, along with the kitchen help—the Three Stooges.

The second insult came when Roger began to spout his version of the Dairy Shack's philosophy.

"Welcome to Team Dairy Shack," Roger said. "You have volunteered for the most intensive fast-food training known to man..."

As the manager spoke, he marched up and down the line, staring into the face of each of his four employees.

"Many of you will not successfully negotiate this program. For those, the shame will be great..."

As Roger droned on, his march became a swagger. "Those of you who succeed will be part of the burger elite."

The stocky guy, whom Matt had nick-named Curly, whispered to the guy next to him. "Isn't this speech in *G.I. Jane?*"

The guy with the wild red hair, whom Matt dubbed Larry, squawked back, "I don't know. *G.I. Jane* was rated R, so my mom didn't let me watch it."

"Quiet, you two!" Roger barked.

The Three Stooges jumped. Curly looked at Matt, then at Roger. He raised his hand timidly.

"What is it, soldier?" Roger said.

"Shouldn't *all* the members of the burger elite wear a uniform?" Curly asked, nodding towards Matt. *Moron*, Matt thought.

"Yeah," Larry put in. "Isn't that how we identify other members of the burger elite?" The third guy nodded in agreement.

Matt refused to let the Stooges gang up on him. "I was hired with the understanding that I *didn't* have to wear a uniform," he said.

Roger nodded. "That sounds like Terri." He glared hard at Matt. "But there's a new sheriff in town tonight. And the new sheriff *likes* the uniform."

Roger tapped Matt's chest.

"*With* the hat," he added.

Matt rolled his eyes.

"Remember, soldier," the night manager went on, "I'm the bossman at the Dairy Shack."

Time to shift strategies, Matt decided.

"Are you paying mileage?" he demanded. "How about insurance? It's my car, you know. What about wear and tear on the automobile?"

Roger was clearly taken aback.

"You have a point," he conceded.

Just then, the Three Stooges all spoke up at once. "We can drive!" they cried.

With mutiny on his hands, Roger knew he had to regain authority. He whirled around to face Matt again.

"You *will* wear the uniform, Camden," he announced. "They're in the kitchen closet."

Matt strode angrily away toward the kitchen.

"And don't forget the *hat,* buster!" Roger called after him.

Mary waved off the waiter again. She didn't have much money, and she didn't want to place an order until Wilson arrived. Where was he, anyway?

Mary checked the neon-lit clock that hung over the corner pool table. It was after eight o'clock.

She scanned the crowded hangout. There was no sign of Wilson.

This is not good, Mary thought.

She had specifically promised Lucy that she'd be gone only an hour or so. If Wilson didn't show soon, she would have to get home before her absence was discovered.

I'll give him fifteen more minutes, she decided. *Then I split. And I'll never speak to Wilson again as long as he lives...*

"Delivery up!" Roger cried.

Matt threw down the greasy towel.

"Action at last!" he muttered.

He stepped away from the sink and headed for the takeout counter.

"I need a delivery boy *now!*" Roger called more urgently.

"Hold your horses," Matt said disgustedly. "I'm coming."

But he was stopped short at the swinging door when he stumbled into Curly.

"Here!" Matt said, stuffing his messy apron into Curly's sweaty palm. "You finish up the pots and pans."

"But it's not my job," Curly whined.

"Do what he says!" Roger barked. "I need a delivery boy. Pronto!"

As Matt reported to Roger, Curly reluctantly put on the apron and went to work.

"I've got an order for two Dairy Burgers, two super big fries, and a chocolate shake," Roger announced, stuffing a warm bag in Matt's hand. "It all comes to $9.96."

Matt checked the address. "This is way out on Pimlico Road," he said.

"It's within our delivery area," Roger countered.

"Just barely!" Matt said.

"Mr. Carter is one of the Dairy Shack's best customers," Roger said.

"You know," Matt said, "even if this guy tips me the usual twenty percent, it won't pay for my gas getting out there."

"That's not the Dairy Shack's problem," Roger said smoothly. "Now is it?"

Then he gave Matt an evil grin. "We're being more than generous with your salary, Mr. Camden. As far as your gas money is concerned..." He paused. "Well, what do you think your minimum wage is *for*?"

Matt threw up his hands and took off. As he exited the front door, he could hear Larry and Curly snickering behind him.

*   *   *

Mrs. Camden lay across her bed. She wished she could put a pillow over her head, but she knew it would hurt her son's feelings.

The song is nearly over, she told herself.

But instead of wrapping up, Simon launched into a second chorus, this time even louder. His singing was punctuated by the cries of both twins.

"Oh, when the saints...go marching in..."

She had to admire Simon's energy. He was giving it his all, and he was just trying to help.

"Oh, how I want to be...in that number..." Simon sang on.

But just as he was about to launch into a third chorus, Samuel and David began to cry even harder.

Simon was genuinely surprised by the twins' reaction.

"I don't get it," he said, sagging on the bed. "I thought since that was *my* favorite song, it would work for David and Samuel."

"Yes," Mrs. Camden replied. "I know. Listen, I appreciate your trying, but—"

Before she could finish, Rev. Camden

entered the bedroom. He was surprised to see Simon bothering his mother and keeping the twins awake.

"Simon, what are you doing here?" he asked. "Didn't you know your mom was going to try to take a nap?"

Mrs. Camden pointed to the screaming twins. "There's not much sleep to be gotten just now. Simon was trying to help."

"Right," Rev. Camden replied. He put an arm around Simon's shoulders. "Sorry, son. How about if us guys take those guys out in the hall and pace for a little while?"

Simon looked up at his father with newfound respect. "Good call, Dad," he said. "That's right out of *Twins: The Terror and the Joy*."

"No, Simon," Rev. Camden said. "It comes from *Camden's Book of Long, Hard Experience!*"

Mrs. Camden rubbed her forehead. "You know what?" she said brightly. "I really don't feel so tired right now. If *both* of you leave, I think I can handle things."

She looked at her husband. *Please get him out of here* was her unspoken command. Rev. Camden got it.

"Whatever you think is best, honey," he replied, pushing Simon ahead of him.

"Oh, Eric!" Mrs. Camden called after them. Her husband stuck his head through the door again.

"Tell Mary and Lucy that the kitchen floor is theirs," Mrs. Camden said. "And the bathtub, too," she added.

Rev. Camden hesitated. "Mary's not back yet."

Mrs. Camden rolled her eyes. "Then put Lucy to work," she said.

"Is that fair?" Rev. Camden asked.

"No," his wife replied. "So here's how we work it. If she admits that Mary ducked out, get her to do just the kitchen floor. But if she covers for her sister—"

"—then I get to put her through the wringer!" Rev. Camden concluded.

Mrs. Camden smiled and nodded.

"See," Rev. Camden said. "Two new babies in the house, and we still have time to torture the other five. I told you this would be fun."

When he left, Mrs. Camden looked down at her twins.

"You both look so tired," she offered. "What do you say to the three of us taking a fifteen- or twenty-minute nap? When we wake up, we'll all feel so refreshed."

David gagged, then continued to wail.

Samuel didn't even take a breath between sobs.

"I'm only thinking of you here," their mother insisted.

But the babies continued to cry and cry.

Lucy listened to the phone ringing on the other end of the line. No one answered.

She gave up and dialed another friend's number. Then she plopped backward onto her bed, waiting for an answer. The phone rang four times before a machine came on.

"No. Not again!" Lucy muttered.

There was a knock on her bedroom door. Lucy hung up as her father entered the room.

"No one is home!" Lucy announced dramatically. "And I mean *no one.*"

"And?" Rev. Camden asked.

"And it's Friday night—Date Night, U.S.A.—and I'm the only one who's sitting at home!"

Rev. Camden smiled. "You mean, you and *Mary.*"

"What?" Lucy said, distracted.

"You *and* Mary. You're the only *two* who don't have dates tonight."

Lucy's mouth snapped shut.

"Yes! Of course! Right!" she stammered nervously. "We—me *and* Mary—*we* don't have dates tonight."

The Reverend looked around the girls' bedroom. "Where is Mary, anyway?" he asked innocently.

Lucy blinked, then looked around herself. "Gee," she replied finally. "She was just here. She must be in the bathroom."

Time to twist the knife, Rev. Camden decided.

"No," he said, shaking his head. "There's no one in the bathroom. I was just there."

"Oh!" Lucy replied, clearly taken by surprise. "Then I guess she must be downstairs."

Rev. Camden nodded. "Must be."

"Why do you ask?" Lucy asked. It was a fatal miscalculation.

"Oh, no reason," her father replied. "Mom just wanted you both to mop the kitchen floor, do some laundry, and scrub the upstairs bathroom."

Lucy's face fell. That was more than enough work for *three* people.

"But," Rev. Camden added, "between the two of you, that shouldn't be *too* hard, should it?"

Lucy, feeling sick, shook her head. "No," she muttered weakly.

"Thank you, hon," Rev. Camden replied a little too sweetly.

When the bedroom door closed behind him, Lucy pounded her bed with her fists.

"Mary will *pay* for this!" she vowed.

Matt stood by his car and listened to the snarling of the big black dog. The animal's dark eyes were fixed on him. Matt decided to give it a few minutes before he tried to make his delivery.

He leaned against the car and studied the house. This end of Pimlico Road was far from the center of town and the lights of the city. The night was pitch-black.

He studied the house at the end of the broad front yard. The porch light was on, as if they expected company—or a delivery. There was a light on inside the house, too. And a dented pickup truck—complete with gun rack—was parked in the driveway.

Matt checked the address again. *Yep,* he decided. *This is the place.*

He waited for another minute, arms crossed, hardly moving.

Finally, the dog, a vicious-looking brute

with long white fangs, curled up in front of its doghouse and rested its wedge-shaped head on the ground. But Matt knew that the beast was still alert—just waiting for him to make a move.

Once more into the breach, Matt thought, recalling a line from his Shakespeare class. He screwed up his courage and crept to the front gate.

The dog was on its feet in an instant. It ran straight at Matt, jaws slavering.

He stepped backward, sure that the dog would tear him apart. But just before the animal reached him, a chain around its neck caught it short.

Matt swallowed hard.

"Hello!" he called. "Mr. Carter? Is anybody home?"

But Mr. Carter, if he was in there, didn't hear him.

What am I going to do now? Matt wondered.

He studied the yard again. Suddenly, he had an idea. The dog's chain didn't quite reach the front porch, but it did reach the main gate.

Matt ignored the dog's cold gaze as he walked casually along the road, parallel to the house. The dog stalked him from the other side of the fence, its chain rattling with every step.

Matt slowed as he neared the porch. The dog was still watching him. Matt walked past the porch, then out of sight behind some high bushes.

When he was sure the dog couldn't see him any more, Matt doubled back.

With a quick, smooth motion, he bounded over the tall hedges surrounding the house and bolted for the front porch. He heard a savage snarl of rage.

The dog had spotted him! But it was too late. Matt was already halfway to the house. He redoubled his efforts, heart pounding.

Finally, he reached the porch—at the same time the black dog ran out of leash. The chain was pulled taut as the dog barked its frustration.

"Missed me!" Matt called. The dog snarled back.

Suddenly, the front door to the house flew open. A tattooed man with a dirty T-shirt, baggy pants, and a cigar stump sticking out of his mouth stared at Matt as if he were from another planet.

"You from Dairy Shack?" the man

asked. Matt nodded. The man pulled the cigar from his thick lips and scratched his stubble.

"Uh, are you Mr. Carter?" Matt stammered.

The man didn't answer. He looked past Matt, at the barking dog in the yard.

"Shut up, Terror!" he shouted. At the sound of his booming voice, the dog's jaw snapped shut. With a whimper, the animal slunk timidly back into its doghouse.

"Took you long enough," the man complained. Matt handed him the bag.

"That will be nine ninety-six, please," Matt said.

The man ignored him. Instead, he opened the bag and plunged one beefy fist into it. He came up gripping a handful of greasy fries, which he stuffed into his mouth. He chewed loudly, wheezing around his food.

Matt looked away.

The tattooed man fumbled in his pocket for a moment and came up with a ten-dollar bill. He stuck it in Matt's fist.

"Thanks, kid," he said. "I love your paper hat."

Before Matt could reply, the man stepped back through his front door and slammed it in Matt's startled face.

As Matt stood there, staring at his four-lousy-cents tip, the porch light went out. Matt was plunged into total darkness. He waited until his eyes grew accustomed to the night before he moved again.

Then he cautiously stepped off the porch.

Almost instantly, a dark streak began racing toward him from the direction of the doghouse.

Matt burst into a run, bolting for the hedges, with Terror nipping at his heels.

FIVE

Mary's mouth dropped open in shock. Standing in front of her table was the last person she had expected to see tonight.

Her little sister's ex-boyfriend.

Mary tried to appear casual as Jordan stood before her, hands thrust into his pockets. His thick blond mane was combed back, away from his intense bright blue eyes. And he was smiling.

Why am I so nervous? Mary thought. *It's just Jordan, for Pete's sake.*

"Hey, Mary! I guess you're surprised to see me." Jordan's voice was soft and sweet. "Are you alone?"

"No!" Mary answered, rather too quickly. "I'm...I'm meeting someone. Um, an ex-boyfriend someone," she clarified.

"Oh," Jordan said, looking around. Mary looked down at her hands.

Anywhere but at Jordan.

But even though she avoided his gaze, Mary could *feel* Jordan's presence.

"So how are the new babies?" Jordan asked, trying to fill the awkward silence.

"They're great," Mary answered, "But very, very loud."

Jordan nodded sympathetically. Then he sat down in the chair across from her. Suddenly, Eddie's felt very warm.

"I'm kind of sorry Lucy and I didn't stick it out a little longer," Jordan said. "I'd love to meet the newest Camdens."

Mary knew he was looking for an invitation. But somehow she couldn't get the words out. *What would Lucy think?* she wondered.

"You know, I have a lot of respect for Lucy," he went on.

"Yeah?" Mary said nervously.

"She always tries so hard to do the right thing. We were both really struggling to make our relationship work—but maybe it shouldn't have worked out in the first place."

Jordan paused. Mary was getting more and more uncomfortable with the direction the conversation was taking.

"The thing about Lucy is that she's so honest. She taught me a lot about telling the truth."

Mary began to squirm. Fortunately, the waiter returned to her table just then.

"I see your date has arrived," he said.

Jordan smiled, enjoying the situation.

"Oh, um…no," Mary replied. "I mean, we're not together. He's not with me." Her voice trailed off.

Jordan came to her rescue.

"Come on," he urged. "Let me buy you a date-free burger while you wait for your *real* date."

Mary hesitated, then nodded. *If Wilson shows up, I'm dead,* she thought. But she smiled and said, "Thanks, that'd be great."

"Two burgers and an order of fries." Jordan told the waiter.

"Coming right up," the waiter said.

Then he was gone, and Mary and Jordan were alone once again.

Mary's heart fluttered as panic rose inside of her once again. Jordan was just too nice—and way too cute!

And he's also Lucy's ex-boyfriend, Mary reminded herself.

*   *   *

Ruthie was in her room, sorting through her stuff. Most of her very favorite toys were spread across her bed. She was packing them into a suitcase.

She held up her majorette baton and studied it. The tassels were worn and many of them were missing.

With a shrug, she tossed the baton in the suitcase. She added her toothbrush and her soft red cloth bag shaped like a car.

Next, she crossed the room to her dresser. She grabbed a framed photograph of Happy and tucked it under her arm. Then she picked up a photo of Simon.

With a toss of her thick, curly hair, Ruthie placed Simon's picture back on top of the dresser.

"I won't be needing *that*," she muttered.

Rev. Camden was passing in the hallway when he peeked into Ruthie's bedroom. He spotted the suitcase and immediately knew something was up. He stepped into the bedroom.

"Where are you going?" he asked.

Ruthie threw a rag doll on top of the growing pile. "As far away from those screaming lumps of snails and puppy dog tails as I can get!"

"You know," her father said, "it's tough

traveling at night. It's dark, and scary, and there are all sorts of creatures out there that can scare just about anyone."

He touched Ruthie's cheek. "Even someone as mature as *you* are."

Ruthie pulled away from her dad.

"I think I have an idea," Rev. Camden offered, as if the thought had just occurred to him. "Why don't you wait until morning to hit the road? It will be bright and sunny and maybe we'll even go together."

"I can't wait until morning!" Ruthie cried. "I have to get some sleep. And I can't with those crying babies around!"

Rev. Camden nodded. "I see your point."

Ruthie continued packing. Her father watched her for a few moments. "So where are you planning to sleep?" he asked.

"In a tree!" Ruthie replied.

"A tree?" Rev. Camden asked.

"Yes," Ruthie explained, her patience wearing thin. "That way, the wild animals won't be able to eat me."

"Ah," Rev. Camden said, nodding. He picked up one of Ruthie's jump ropes and stuck it inside the bulging suitcase.

"What's *that* for?" Ruthie asked.

"I was just thinking that you'd better tie

yourself to a branch or something. That way you won't fall and hurt yourself."

Ruthie scratched her chin. "Good suggestion," she said. "Thanks!"

"Well," Rev. Camden said finally, "I've got things to do"—he pointed to Ruthie's suitcase—"and I can see that you do, too."

Ruthie nodded.

"Okay," Rev. Camden said casually as he walked into the hallway. "Give me a holler when you're on your way."

"Right!" Ruthie cried, throwing up her hands. "Like you'll be able to hear me with all of the racket around here."

Out in the hall, her father sighed.

How do I deal with this? he wondered.

Just then, Simon came out of his room. He was clutching yet another child care book. His father grabbed him.

"Do me a favor," he begged. "Do not, under any circumstances, let Ruthie out of your sight."

"What's up?"

"She's planning to run away."

"She *told* you that?" Simon asked.

"Yes."

Simon shook his blond head. "Ruthie's so bad at this kind of thing."

"Fortunately, your sister isn't exactly

subtle," Rev. Camden agreed. "So your mission is to keep your eye on her at all times."

"You *do* see that she's just a confused little girl, bewildered by all the sudden changes in this family," Simon insisted. "She's really crying out for attention."

Rev. Camden looked at his son. "I take it you got that out of a book," he said.

"Don't change the subject!" Simon told his father.

"Okay," Rev. Camden replied. "Yes, I *do* see all of those things. And your mom and I are doing everything we can to give Ruthie the attention she needs."

His son looked up at him doubtfully.

"But right now," Rev. Camden went on, "we have our hands full and we'd like *you* to give her some of *your* attention. *All* of your attention. Got it?"

"Sure," Simon said with a shrug. "I'm a team player."

Rev. Camden smiled. "I'm delighted to hear that."

"Hey, Dad," Simon called after him. "Are you hungry?"

"I'm too tired to be hungry." Rev. Camden said, his shoulders sagging.

"If I pay for it, can I order a pizza or something?" asked Simon.

"Or something?" his father said.

Simon shrugged, trying to look innocent. "I don't know exactly what my taste buds are in the mood for yet."

"If you and your taste buds are thinking of giving the Dairy Shack a jingle, forget it," Rev. Camden said. "I don't want Matt to think that we're checking up on him."

"But what if the pizza place isn't delivering tonight?" Simon insisted.

"Now what are the odds of that?" Rev. Camden asked.

"These are strange times, Dad," Simon replied seriously. "It *could* happen."

"No," Rev. Camden said. "It couldn't." But he was tired, impatient, and overwhelmed. He conceded defeat.

"Simon," he said, "do what you think is right."

Simon smiled in triumph.

That was easy, he told himself.

Rev. Camden had just put his hand on the doorknob when Lucy came up.

"Hey, Dad, have you seen Mary?"

"No," he replied. "But I haven't been downstairs lately. Should we go down there together and find her?"

Lucy suddenly looked like a trapped animal.

"*No!*" she cried. "I mean, you don't have to bother. *I'll* find Mary."

"Great!" Rev. Camden said with a satisfied smile. "Then you two can get started."

"Get started?" Lucy repeated blankly.

"You know," Rev. Camden reminded her. "The kitchen floor. The bathroom. The rest of the laundry…"

"Oh, yeah, right!" Lucy said.

"Your mother and I really appreciate this," Rev. Camden said. "And—"

"I know, I know!" Lucy interrupted, raising one hand. "You're welcome."

After her father went into his bedroom, Lucy gritted her teeth. "Just wait until I get my hands on Mary," she muttered.

The wail of angry babies greeted Rev. Camden as he entered the bedroom. His wife turned to him, her look haggard.

"I can't believe it!" she cried. "If I get one of them quieted down, the other one starts crying. It's like a tag team!"

"Things will get better," Rev. Camden promised lamely. But his wife knew she didn't have his undivided attention.

"What's going on?" she demanded.

"Nothing," Rev. Camden said. But he withered under his wife's gaze.

"Well, we've got Ruthie problems," he admitted.

"I know," Mrs. Camden said, sighing.

"And Simon is ordering some food," Rev. Camden continued. "I think he's planning to call the Dairy Shack. They deliver now, you know."

Mrs. Camden nodded. "I'd heard that. But you aren't going to let Simon humiliate Matt on his first night at work, are you?"

Rev. Camden shrugged. "I'm not *letting* him do anything."

"Oh, I see," Mrs. Camden replied. "We've got two new sons, so you're just going to let the two we already have get out of control?"

Rev. Camden pointed to his chest. "*Me?*" he asked innocently.

Mrs. Camden put her hands on her hips. "You are such a cruel man!" she said, her eyes twinkling.

David and Samuel let loose with a new chorus of wailing.

"Here we go again," Mrs. Camden sighed. She and her husband each chose a cradle and began rocking.

*   *   *

"What do *you* want?" Ruthie demanded, eyeing her older brother suspiciously.

"I know what you're planning," Simon informed her. "And I'm here to help," he announced.

"Fine," Ruthie said. "Get me the other suitcase. It's in the closet."

"That's not what I meant," Simon said. "Stupid stunts like running away never work on Mom and Dad. Trust me, they've seen it all. They had *me* before they had you."

"They had *both* of us before they had the twins," Ruthie added glumly.

"It's just a phase parents go through," Simon explained. "It's like when you get a new toy and forget about the old ones."

Ruthie considered Simon's words.

"Here's an example," he continued. "If somebody gave you a brand-new silver Red Lightning ring, you'd forget all about your old, broken Princess Greenstone bracelet."

Ruthie frowned. "You're saying that I'm an old piece of junk."

Simon shook his head. "I think you're missing the point."

"Whatever!" Ruthie cried, throwing up her hands.

"Here." Simon pulled a small, bright

object out of his pocket. "I want you to have this."

He handed the prize over to his sister.

"Wow," Ruthie gasped. "Your lucky Red Lightning ring. Thanks!"

"You're welcome." Simon held Ruthie's shoulders. "I want you to do something for me," he asked.

Ruthie nodded.

"Every time you look at that ring, remember what I said. And try to give Mom and Dad a break."

Ruthie nodded again.

Well, that was easy, Simon told himself smugly. *Maybe I'll write a baby book myself.*

"Hey, want to order something from the Dairy Shack?" he asked.

"No thanks," Ruthie said, trying on the ring.

Simon shrugged. "Your loss," he said as he headed toward the phone in the den.

Ruthie took off the ring and rubbed it clean with the hem of her jumper. When it was as shiny as she could make it, she carefully tucked it inside the suitcase with the rest of her stuff.

Matt blinked in the relentless glare of the policeman's flashlight. A dark silhouette studied him. Matt kept his eyes forward.

"Camden?" a gruff voice asked, sounding surprised. "Is that *you*, Matt?"

Oh, no, Matt thought.

He turned to face the police officer. The flashlight suddenly shifted, and Matt could see the man's face.

"Uh, hello, Sergeant Richards," Matt stammered. "Nice night, isn't it?"

Ben Richards and his family were active members of his father's church.

That only made things worse.

"What are you doing out here on the wrong end of Pimlico Road?" the policeman demanded. "And driving *above* the speed limit?"

"It's my new job," Matt explained. "I work for—"

"Let me guess," Sgt. Richards smiled. "The Dairy Shack."

Matt nodded.

"First night?"

Matt nodded again.

"Well, I'm going to let you off with a warning," the officer said sternly. "But not because I know your father, either!"

Sgt. Richards adjusted his gun belt and leaned against Matt's Camaro.

"Nope," the policeman continued. "I'm

letting you off with a warning because you were only going five miles over the limit...and because I know Roger Denbro."

"You mean Dairy Shack Roger?" Matt said. "My boss Roger?"

"Yeah," Sgt. Richards nodded. "I've known him since he was a kid. And I figure that anybody who could work for that guy deserves all the breaks he can get."

Matt breathed a sigh of relief. "Uh, thanks a lot, Sergeant," he said.

Sgt. Richards chuckled. "That sure is a stupid uniform."

"Can I go?" Matt asked finally. This was getting to be too much to take.

"Sure, go on," Sgt. Richards said, waving him off. "Get back to work. But do your delivering at the speed limit, okay?"

Matt nodded and started the car.

"Hey, Camden!" the officer called from beside his squad car.

Matt leaned out the window.

"Nice hat!"

Matt kept his eyes front and his mouth shut as he drove away.

"Wow, this looks absolutely delicious," Mary said when the waiter arrived with her and Jordan's food. The waiter set a plate heaped with hot fries and charcoal-broiled burgers in front of them.

"Enjoy," Jordan said.

As they ate, Mary began to relax. Eddie's was really hopping now, and several Centerville students had set up a spontaneous arm-wrestling competition.

Watching all the kids having a good time, Mary suddenly realized how seldom she'd gone out since she and Wilson had stopped seeing each other. It also occurred to her that she'd been pining for Wilson too long. She was letting life pass her by.

As Jordan watched the arm wrestlers, Mary watched him. She was actually having a lot of fun with Lucy's ex. So much fun, in fact, that she was beginning to wonder why Lucy had dumped Jordan in the first place.

"So how was your burger?" Jordan asked.

"Wonderful!" Mary declared. "Best meal I've had in days, believe me."

"Maybe you should come here more often," Jordan suggested.

Mary nodded. But she was a little disappointed that Jordan hadn't said "*We* should come here more often."

Jordan picked up an unused napkin

and began to fold it into a paper football.

Mary made a goalpost with her hands. Jordan kicked off, and a furious game of finger football began.

"Goal!" Jordan cried a moment later as his tiny football sailed easily over Mary's fingers. He threw his muscular arms above his head in mock triumph.

"Pretty sweet," Mary agreed. "Now hand over that football. It's *my* turn to kick off!"

Mary was having so much fun with Jordan that she didn't even notice that it was almost nine o'clock. And that her real date for the evening was almost an hour late.

SIX

Simon sat in the den, leaning comfortably back in a chair. The phone was in his lap. In his hands he clutched the Dairy Shack delivery menu. As he scanned the selections, Simon anticipated the pleasure he would soon experience.

But not from one of the Dairy Shack's many wholesome and delicious fast-food items. Simon was anticipating the joy of tormenting his older brother. He made his choices and dialed the phone, propping his feet on the desk.

Roger's high-pitched voice answered. "Hello! Welcome to the Dairy Shack, offering fast service from courteous drivers bringing you hot and delicious Dairy Shack lunches, dinners, and snacks. May I take your order, please?"

"Certainly," Simon replied. "This is the Camden residence." He gave Roger his address and phone number. "I'd like a chili cheese dog with onions."

"Very good, sir," Roger replied. Then Simon heard a familiar voice in the background.

"Could you wait one moment?" Roger asked politely.

"Of course," Simon said, smiling.

"Where have you been?" Roger barked when Matt returned to the Dairy Shack. Matt didn't reply.

Roger grew livid.

"I asked you a question, Camden! And as your boss, I expect an answer!"

He held the phone away from him. But still, he could hear his customer laughing on the other end of the line.

Roger put the receiver back to his mouth. "May I put you on hold?" he asked.

Then he swung back to Matt.

"Where were you?" he demanded.

"Delivering orders," Matt said.

"Well, you're too slow!" Roger cried. "We're losing business here!"

"Too *slow?*" Matt said loudly, his outrage beginning to spill over his control. "You sent me all the way out to Pimlico Road, where I had to face Cujo the Killer Dog—just to deliver a burger and some fries!"

"Drive a little faster," Roger said.

"Faster!" Matt sputtered. "I already got pulled over by a cop for speeding!"

Roger stared at Matt, appalled. "Did you get a ticket?" he demanded.

Matt shook his head. "Sergeant Richards let me off with a warning."

"Well, just make sure that warning sticks, buster!" Roger said threateningly. "The Dairy Shack does not tolerate fast or unsafe drivers. A ticket could have jeopardized your career in fast food."

Matt opened his mouth. He'd had it. It was time to really give it to Roger the Tyrant. Matt knew it would feel great. At least he would regain his dignity.

But Matt also knew that losing his temper would cost him his job. There was also the matter of that bet with his father.

He snapped his mouth shut.

Calm down, he ordered himself. *Just take a deep breath and count to ten.*

Matt counted all the way up to twenty-five before he was finally ready to face his boss again. He swallowed his pride.

"Sorry, Roger," Matt said flatly. "I'll do better next time."

Roger Denbro looked triumphant.

"Don't look so superior, Roger," Matt added. "I was only gone twenty-five minutes or so."

The manager's face reddened. Matt couldn't resist one more dig.

"Loosen up your bow tie, Roger," Matt suggested. "It looks like it might be a little tight."

"What did you say?" Roger demanded.

"Just remember," Matt replied sweetly. "Without me, you wouldn't have anyone driving anything anywhere tonight...I'm the only person around here with a car."

"Fine!" Roger squealed. "But just you remember who the bossman is around here, buster!"

Then he turned his attention back to the phone call.

"That's a chili cheese dog with onions. Anything else with that, sir?" Roger said.

Matt went to the sink and washed his hands, imagining all sorts of ways to get even with his night manager.

Behind him, the delivery phone rang again.

*   *   *

Rev. Camden listened to the phone ring on the other end of the line. Finally, he heard a click.

"Hello!" a voice squeaked. "Welcome to the Dairy Shack, offering fast service from courteous drivers bringing you hot and delicious Dairy Shack lunches, dinners, and snacks. May I put you on hold?"

"Absolutely," Rev. Camden replied.

Then he looked back at his wife with a conspiratorial grin. "This second line is coming in handy, eh?"

Mrs. Camden smiled. "Don't get used to it," she replied. "We're getting rid of it next week."

"Thank you for holding!" Roger apologized when he returned to the line. "May I take your order, please?"

Downstairs in the kitchen, Lucy was waxing the floor—her way.

A boom box shook the kitchen table. It was tuned to a hard-rock station, and the volume was pumped up loud.

While the radio blared, Lucy flew back and forth across the kitchen, pushing a mop in front of her. And she never missed a spot on the expansive floor—since she was wearing cleaning rags under her feet!

When the song ended, Lucy swung around to find Ruthie watching her.

Ruthie was wearing woolen pajamas, and her tiny feet were tucked snugly into her favorite bunny slippers.

But she had also donned her thick blue winter coat and a long, matching scarf. She wore a wool hat, and a pair of earmuffs were tangled crookedly in her thick hair.

But the strangest thing of all was that she carried an overstuffed suitcase with one hand and clutched a long jump rope in the other.

Lucy switched off the boom box.

"So," she said casually, "where are *you* off to?"

Ruthie blinked up at Lucy. "I've had it with this place!" she declared.

Just then, Simon raced down the steps and grabbed Ruthie.

"Can't you wait one lousy little second before you go anywhere?" he demanded. "Give me a break!"

But Ruthie wouldn't be herded by Simon. "If you two had any sense, you'd come with me!" she cried.

Lucy and Simon exchanged looks.

"She's got a point," Lucy conceded.

"Yeah," Simon agreed, sighing. "I *hate* when that happens."

"Delivery up!" Roger cried.

Matt, who'd just finished washing another stack of dishes, rolled his eyes. Behind him, Larry and Curly snickered.

Matt went to the front of the eatery and reported to Roger. The night manager thrust two bags into Matt's hand.

"Here's the address," he announced. Matt took the paper from Roger's hand.

Oh, no, he thought. *Simon.* But Matt grew suspicious when he saw the size of the delivery. He checked the receipt. One bag contained two grilled chicken sandwiches. That meant Simon was not alone in his conspiracy.

Grilled chicken sandwiches were Rev. Camden's favorite food.

Ruthie was still trying to convince Lucy and Simon that their best chance was escape. Their argument was growing more animated when Mrs. Camden came down the stairs.

"What's all the excitement about?" she asked, rubbing her temples.

"Sorry, Mom," Lucy said. "We didn't

mean to wake you up."

Mrs. Camden smiled weakly. "That would mean I would have actually been *asleep* at some point," she said. She glanced down at the rags under Lucy's feet. "The sock and mop?" she said, raising one eyebrow. "Was that Mary's idea?"

Lucy paled. Mrs. Camden pressed her advantage. "So where *is* your sister?

Lucy looked like a trapped animal.

"I...I don't know!" Lucy stammered. "I mean, I'm really not sure. She was just in here a minute ago."

"I can tell," Mrs. Camden said with a nod. "The kitchen floor is so shiny and clean that you couldn't possibly have done it all by yourself."

She ran her foot across the slippery linoleum. "And is that a fresh coat of wax?" she asked.

Lucy nodded.

"Boy!" Mrs. Camden continued. "That Mary can really work wonders."

Then she spotted the bag of dirty laundry. "Shouldn't you be doing that?"

Lucy gulped. "I guess so," she replied.

"Well, get to work," Mrs. Camden said. She turned her attention to her youngest daughter, eyeing Ruthie's coat, the suitcase, and the jump rope. "What's *your* story?"

"Um, I just took out the trash?" Ruthie lied.

"Uh-huh," Mrs. Camden said skeptically. "With a suitcase?"

Ruthie looked down at her feet. Mrs. Camden lifted the little girl's chin.

"If you leave," she told her, "you're supposed to *tell* someone."

Ruthie nodded.

"But I really, really hope you stay," Mrs. Camden continued. "Because if you don't, I will be very sad and scared for you out there all alone in the cold dark night."

Ruthie considered her mother's words.

"Do us both a favor," Mrs. Camden begged. "Go upstairs and wait until morning before you run away."

"Fine!" Ruthie cried. "Tonight or tomorrow, I'm out of here, no matter what." She bolted up the stairs.

Mrs. Camden looked at Simon.

"Go up there right now and keep an eye on Ruthie," she commanded.

"You know she's crying out for help," Simon began.

Mrs. Camden's patience was at an end. It was time to stop humoring Simon's child-rearing enthusiasms.

"Don't you dare let her out of your sight!" she said. "Not for one second!"

"Okay, I'm going, I'm going," Simon said, following his little sister.

Then Mrs. Camden turned her gaze on Lucy once again.

"Well!" Lucy said brightly. "I guess I'd better get a load of laundry in."

"Yep," her mother said, hands on hips.

"And then I'll go upstairs and start scrubbing that bathroom," Lucy added.

Mrs. Camden smiled. "If I know Mary, she's probably already started."

Ha! Lucy thought.

"Boy, can she scrub a tub," Mrs. Camden went on. She patted Lucy on the back and went back up the stairs.

When her mother was gone, Lucy put the mop back into the closet. Then she dumped the rags into the bulging laundry bag and threw the bag over her shoulders.

Bent double by the weight, Lucy headed for the laundry room. Every step of the way, she vowed to make Mary pay!

Jordan flipped another paper football over Mary's raised thumbs.

"Goal!" he cried.

Mary shook her head. "I'm half-impressed and half-scared by how good you are at this game."

Jordan sat back and smiled, basking in the glow of his third consecutive victory.

Mary's eyes wandered to the neon clock on the wall. She blinked when she saw the time.

"Yikes! I'd better get going," she said.

"What about your date?" Jordan reminded her.

Mary shrugged. "I guess he stood me up." *And I don't even care,* she added to herself.

"Are you sure?"

Mary nodded. "I've really got to get home," she said.

"Sure," Jordan agreed. "You don't want to miss out on any of that crying."

Mary considered his words. "While you have a very good point, I really must get out of here."

"Why?" Jordan asked.

"Well, for one thing, Lucy is at home covering for me. It's not exactly her best skill," Mary explained.

Jordan nodded. "It's her honesty thing again," he said.

"Who knows how long she can keep up the lie under pressure?" Mary said. "She caves easily."

"Yeah. Well in that case, I think it's safe to assume that your parents already know you've gone AWOL," Jordan said. "They'd probably be on their way over right now, except for one thing—"

Mary sighed. "The babies are still crying," she finished.

Jordan nodded. "Exactly," he said.

Mary smiled happily and picked up the paper football.

"Okay!" she declared. "You win. But this time I get to kick off first!"

"I really wouldn't ask you to do this, Lucy, but it's *oh* so important," Lucy rambled on in a pretty fair imitation of Mary.

She paused to furiously attack a stubborn patch of soap scum.

"Wilson wants to see me *oh* so much, Lucy, and I'll only be gone an hour! One teeny-weeny little hour."

Lucy snorted and threw the sponge into the tub. "Like she can't get a *new* boyfriend anytime she wants to."

She pushed a lock of hair away from her face and scrubbed some more.

"Mary! Lucy!" Rev. Camden called from the hallway. "Keep up the good work. Remember, cleanliness is next to godliness."

Lucy looked toward the heavens. "Like God cares if our bathtub is clean," she muttered.

"What did you say, Lucy?" Rev. Camden called, closer now. Lucy pushed the bathroom door closed with her toe.

"Nothing, Dad!" she answered. "I was talking to Mary."

"Oh, and girls," Rev. Camden added from the other side of the door, "I noticed that the dryer has stopped. Could one of you run downstairs and unload it before everything gets wrinkled?"

"Help me," Lucy whispered to the heavens again. Then, much louder, she called, "I'll take care of it, Dad."

"Thanks, hon."

Then he was gone, and Lucy breathed a sigh of relief.

She scooped up the sponge, sprayed some cleanser on the wall, and continued to work. Her anger fueled a scrubbing frenzy.

Matt walked up to the door of his own house and rang the bell. He waited in the dark for someone to arrive. He was certain it would be Simon.

Finally the front door opened. Simon grinned at Matt.

"So," he said, crossing his arms, "they make you wear a *hat?*"

Matt yanked the paper hat from his head. He'd forgotten to take it off before his little brother saw it.

"Very nice," Simon taunted. "Is it made of paper?"

Matt sneered.

"You'd better stay away from the grill," Simon advised. "Between that hat and your hair spray, you're a human fireball waiting to happen."

"Very funny," Matt replied, shoving the bags into Simon's arms.

"That'll be seventeen dollars and thirty-five cents," Matt said. "And I'd suggest you add a *big* tip."

Simon's mouth dropped open. "A chili dog costs seventeen bucks?" he cried.

"No," Matt said, shaking his head. "But there was an order added to yours, and all together it comes to seventeen dollars and thirty-five cents. So pay up."

Simon reached into his pocket.

"That price is *excluding* the big tip,"

Matt added. "The big tip that allows you to draw breath for one more day."

He shoved the receipt into Simon's face. Simon took it and began to scan the list. Matt crossed his arms, waiting for his brother to finish.

Just then, Mrs. Camden came around the corner.

"Did I hear the doorbell?" she asked. Then she saw Matt.

"Hey!" She waved. "How's it going?"

Matt smiled weakly.

"*He's* fine!" Simon threw up his hands. He showed the receipt to his mother. "Do *you* know anything about this?"

Mrs. Camden glanced at the receipt. "Yep!" she announced. "That's everything."

Simon rolled his eyes. "And who exactly is going to pay for *everything?*"

"Well," Mrs. Camden replied, "your dad did say that if a pizza came through the door, he would pay for it. Anything else is your treat."

She bent down and kissed Simon's blond hair. "So thank you very much, my gracious, generous son."

Then Mrs. Camden grabbed the larger of the two bags out of Simon's grasp and headed up the stairs.

This is totally unfair!" Simon said.

He turned to his brother for support. Matt held out his palm.

"Pay up!" he repeated.

All the commotion in the foyer drew Ruthie out of her bedroom. She peeked downstairs.

Simon was arguing with Matt. Their mom was coming back upstairs with a Dairy Shack bag in her hands. Ruthie quickly ducked back into her room, until her mother passed.

Ruthie clapped a hand to her mouth to stop herself from laughing. Matt looked *so* dumb in a Dairy Shack uniform!

"I wonder where Lucy and Mary are?" Ruthie whispered. She suddenly realized that no one was around to keep an eye on her.

Mom and Dad were back in their room with the crying babies. Only Happy was around. The dog was waiting by Simon's door with her plastic food bowl.

Ruthie ran back to her room and looked outside. The night was dark, and she couldn't see much. But she did spot Matt's car in the driveway.

"Sweet," she said. "That's my ticket out of this dump!"

Collecting her suitcase, her jump rope, and the flashlight from the hallway closet, Ruthie was off. She slipped quietly down the back stairs.

Behind her, Happy whimpered.

"Go find Simon!" Ruthie hissed. Happy picked up her bowl and scampered off.

Downstairs, Ruthie carefully crossed the darkened kitchen. She opened the back door and crept outside.

The night air was cool, and the suitcase felt very heavy all of a sudden. But Ruthie wrapped her scarf tightly around her neck and pulled her hat down over her ears. With a final look back at the house, she pressed on.

She stood in the shadow of a big tree until she was sure the coast was clear.

Then Ruthie dashed toward Matt's Camaro.

.

Rev. Camden rocked David with one arm and ate a grilled chicken sandwich with the other. As Mrs. Camden fed Samuel, Rev. Camden paced back and forth across the bedroom, trying to calm David's sobs.

Near the window, he peeked between the curtains.

"Honey, come here!" he called to his wife.

"Guess who just got in the back of Matt's car?" Rev. Camden asked.

"Look, I don't have all night," Matt told Simon. "I've got other deliveries to make."

"Hey!" Simon argued. "I'm not just going to eyeball the receipt when we're talking about this kind of money."

Matt changed his extended palm into a claw reaching for his little brother's throat.

Simon got the message immediately. He slapped a twenty-dollar bill into Matt's hand seconds before the claw reached him.

"Thank you," Matt said.

Now it was Simon's turn to extend his palm. "My change?" he demanded.

"My tip?" Matt shot back. Simon folded his arms over his chest.

"You know," he said, "There is a growing belief that tipping is merely subsidizing what the employer should be paying his employees in the first place."

Matt glared at him.

"But I, myself, am on the fence, so…enjoy!"

Simon slammed the door in Matt's face, then locked it, before his older brother could react. He leaned against the solid oak, listening until he heard Matt's retreating footsteps.

A pathetic whimper sounded from below. Simon looked down to see Happy standing on her hind legs, her plastic food bowl in her mouth. The dog's tail was wagging expectantly.

In the upstairs bathroom, Lucy was still in the bathroom, scrubbing soap stains. The water was running in the tub.

As she worked on a really tough spot, Lucy dropped the sponge. She sighed and reached into the tub to retrieve it. She came up with nothing.

Where did it go? she wondered.

She searched in the rising water for the missing sponge.

Wait a minute, Lucy thought, her stomach tight. *Why is the water rising?*

"Oh, no!" she cried, diving for the drain.

Her fingers just brushed the edge of the sponge before it was sucked down the bathtub drain.

With a groan, Lucy shut off the water

and threw a rebellious strand of hair over her shoulders. Carefully, she reached into the drain with her fingers.

The sponge was so far down she couldn't reach it.

Squealing in frustration, Lucy jumped up, splashing water everywhere. She fumbled through the closet under the sink and came up clutching her weapon of choice—the toilet plunger. With a feeling of grim determination, Lucy went to work on the drain.

SEVEN

Matt climbed behind the wheel of his Camaro again, fuming.

He put his paper hat back on top of his head and stuck the keys in the ignition. Then he sensed movement behind him.

Matt reached up and adjusted his rearview mirror.

For some reason, he wasn't that surprised when he saw Ruthie in the back seat. A suitcase was stuffed on the floor between the seats. She clutched a jump rope in one hand, a flashlight in the other.

"You," Matt said, his eyes meeting hers in the mirror. *"Out!"*

"I'd love to ride around in a car full of hamburgers and french fries," Ruthie pleaded.

Matt turned around in the driver's seat and faced his little sister.

"Look," he said patiently, "it's only our first week with the babies. They *are* crying all the time now, but it'll get better."

Ruthie gave him a skeptical look. "Are you kidding?" she cried. "It'll only get *worse!*"

Matt sighed. "Look, Ruthie, just go back inside."

"No!" Ruthie replied stubbornly.

"Don't make me get Mom and Dad," Matt threatened.

"Ha!" Ruthie retorted. "You couldn't get them away from the Children of the Corn even if you wanted to!"

"I tried doing this the nice way," Matt said. "Now I have to do it the *hard* way."

He opened the door and climbed out of the Camaro. The he reached into the back seat to grab Ruthie.

She dived to the opposite side of the car. Matt climbed in the back seat. Soon they were struggling furiously.

"Come on, Ruthie!" Matt begged. "You know you can't go with me. I'm sure it's against some stupid Dairy Shack policy or something!"

"No!" Ruthie screamed, so loud Matt

was sure the whole neighborhood heard her.

She wrapped her arms around the seat belt and held on as tightly as she could. Matt pulled Ruthie's legs until she screamed again.

"Come out, Ruthie!" Matt demanded.

"No way, you big bully! Let me go!"

Lucy pumped the plunger over the plugged drain again and again. More hair, more soap scum, and more chunks of she-didn't-want-to-know-what bubbled up from under the murky water.

But no sponge.

She reached into the drain once again. Her hand came up tangled in a ball of thick, dark hair.

"Ohhh, yuck!" Lucy cried.

Frantically, she began plunging again. Dirty water splashed everywhere, creating a whole new mess.

"Mary," Lucy muttered darkly under her breath. "Mary..."

Simon pulled a can of dog food from the shelf and took it to the counter. Then he took the blue plastic bowl from Happy's mouth. He searched for the can opener in the utility drawer as the dog whimpered.

"Just a minute, girl," Simon said.

Suddenly, he felt a cold draft on his neck. He turned and discovered that the back door was wide open, filling the kitchen with cool night air.

"That's weird," Simon said. He looked down at Happy.

"You're some guard dog," he scolded. "Aren't you supposed to bark or something? What if a burglar came in here?"

Happy whimpered apologetically.

"I wonder how that happened?" Simon pondered as he closed the door.

Then he had a realization. A really *bad* realization.

He threw open the door again.

"Ruthie! I know you're out here somewhere," Simon shouted from the back porch. His voice echoed among the trees.

He crossed the yard and ran up to the Camaro. Matt was still trying to drag Ruthie out of his car.

"No! I won't go back to that house of horror!" Ruthie howled, biting and scratching at Matt's arms. Fortunately, his skin was protected by his thick leather jacket.

"That's it!" Matt cried when Simon arrived. "I've had it! Go get Mom and Dad!"

Simon froze, a guilty expression on his face. "I...I can't," he stammered.

"Why not?" Matt demanded.

"Because if I bring them into this, they'll know that Ruthie escaped," Simon explained. "I'm supposed to be watching her. At all times."

Matt pounded the hood of his car with his fists. "I can't believe this!" he cried angrily. He pushed past his little brother and stormed back up to the house.

In less than a second, Simon was in the back seat of the Camaro with Ruthie.

"Please, Ruthie, pretty, pretty please!" he begged. "Just come back inside the house and we'll talk about all this."

Ruthie's arms remained stubbornly crossed. She refused to budge.

"The only thing I want to talk about is how we send those babies back to wherever they came from," she said firmly.

"They belong to *us* now," Simon said, trying to reason with his sister. "We're supposed to love and cherish them as part of our family."

Ruthie covered her ears.

"I don't care what anybody says," she declared. "Those babies are not cute."

"Of course not," Simon agreed, nodding furiously. "Compared to you, who is?"

Ruthie's expression softened for an instant. Then she frowned again.

"Good try," she told him. "But I'm not buying it. Get away from me."

Simon looked back at the house. So far there was no sign of his parents, but he didn't know how long his luck would hold out.

It was time to bargain.

"I'll give you a cookie?" Simon tried. Ruthie turned up her nose.

"Okay," Simon bargained. "How about cookies and ice cream?"

Ruthie snubbed that offer, too.

Time to go for broke, Simon decided.

"Money?" he said finally. "Cold, hard cash?"

Ruthie gave Simon a disgusted look.

"I liked it better when you were ignoring me," she told him.

The music at Eddie's had gotten so loud that Mary and Jordan couldn't hear their own conversation. Mary used the lull to glance at her watch.

She was shocked when she saw the time. It was nearly ten!

She jumped up to go. Jordan tried to

say something, but his words were lost in the pounding music.

"What?" Mary asked, cupping her ear.

Jordan leaned closer. "I said," he repeated, "would you like to dance?"

As he spoke, his breath brushed Mary's neck. The sensation sent tingles of delight along her spine.

Mary was struck dumb. Before she even thought about it, she nodded.

Gently, Jordan took Mary's hand in his, leading her out to the tiny dance area.

Mesmerized, Mary forgot all about the time—and Wilson—and Lucy.

"*Got* ya!" Lucy cried triumphantly.

With a final tug, she ripped the sponge out of the drain.

Almost immediately, the disgusting dirty water began to subside.

Lucy leaned against the tile, exhausted. Her overalls were wet, her hands were filthy.

But she was victorious.

She had won, and the sponge had lost. Best of all, her mom and dad would never know.

Lucy tossed the shredded sponge into the trash can. Then she wiped her hands on her overalls and scanned the bathroom.

It was a disaster area.

Lucy felt like crying. The bathroom looked worse now than it had before she'd started to clean it.

She jumped at a sudden knock on the door.

"Go away!" she shouted.

"It's just me, honey," Rev. Camden called from the other side of the door. "I was on my way downstairs to take care of Ruthie, and I thought I'd stop by and see how you and Mary were doing."

"Uh...we're doing fine. Just fine. What can I do for you, Dad?" Lucy replied, trying to gather her wits.

"Did I mention the laundry?" Rev. Camden asked innocently. "I'm so tired I, well, I just can't remember. Anyway, it looks like nobody has started on it yet."

The laundry! Lucy slapped her forehead. She'd forgotten all about it.

She took a deep breath. "We're almost done in here," she said brightly. "Then we'll *both* get on that laundry right away."

"Great," Rev. Camden replied. "I really appreciate what both of you are doing."

"Don't mention it, Dad," Lucy said.

Under her breath she added, *"Please* don't mention it. Again. Ever. Or I'll *scream!"*

Matt stood between the two cradles, his Dairy Shack hat in hand. Softly, he sang his favorite hymn to the twins. He gazed at the babies with deep understanding.

And the hope that both of them would just shut up!

He was having about as much luck as everyone else at calming the babies.

Absolutely none.

"I don't get it, Mom," Matt said, looking over his shoulder. "I can't get them to stay quiet for even a nanosecond."

"Nobody can," Mrs. Camden replied. "Those two are as stubborn as the rest of the Camden men."

She dropped back against the pillow and covered her ears. Beside her was a cold grilled chicken sandwich—barely touched.

Suddenly, both babies whimpered and stopped crying.

Matt held his breath. He and his mother exchanged hopeful glances as they listened to the precious sound of silence.

"Well, here she is!" Rev. Camden announced loudly, entering the room with

Ruthie in his arms. At the sound of their father's voice, the twins started to cry again.

"Go," Mrs. Camden told Matt. "Get back to work. I'll handle things from here."

"Thanks, Mom," Matt said gratefully. He left the room like a shot.

Mrs. Camden shot her husband a look of irritation.

"Sorry," he said. "Did I miss something?"

"Never mind," Mrs. Camden replied as she rocked both cradles. Ruthie, still in her father's arms, turned away from her mother and buried her face in Rev. Camden's neck.

"Where's Simon?" he asked.

"I thought he was with you," Mrs. Camden answered. "And why wasn't he watching Ruthie, anyway?"

Ruthie lifted her head. "Is Simon my new mommy?" she murmured.

Mrs. Camden blinked in surprise.

Rev. Camden put his daughter down and Ruthie left the room without a backward glance.

"Well, I've got to clean up," Rev. Camden announced. Then he frowned and held up one foot. His sock was wet and yellow.

"Happy," he told his wife in disgust. "Simon never walked the dog."

Suddenly, all the frustration and exhaustion of the past few days welled up inside of Mrs. Camden. She burst into uncontrollable laughter.

"It's not funny," her husband said with a wounded look.

Mrs. Camden laughed even louder.

"It's really not *that* funny," Rev. Camden insisted, peeling off the wet sock.

Mrs. Camden howled, gasping for breath. Her face was starting to turn red.

Finally, Rev. Camden smiled. Then he started to laugh along with his wife, until tears ran down their cheeks.

Soon, both the twins and their parents were crying.

Mary and Jordan danced through three songs. Then a soft, slow love song came through the jukebox. Mary and Jordan paused for an awkward moment.

Then Jordan smiled. Mary moved closer to him.

He reached out and wrapped a strong arm around Mary's waist. Mary surrendered against his chest.

The song was one of Mary's favorites.

She never imagined she'd actually get to dance to it with Jordan.

She was troubled by the wild emotions she was feeling. But she couldn't deny that it felt great to be in Jordan's arms.

Their eyes met, and Jordan jokingly dipped her toward the floor. When he pulled her up again, Mary laughed.

"You're full of surprises," she said.

Jordan didn't reply. Instead, he pulled Mary close.

With a sigh, Mary rested her chin on his broad shoulder. Together, they drifted as one across the tiny dance floor.

Matt burst out of the house and walked briskly to the car, checking his watch. Now he was in major trouble.

I've been gone way too long, he thought.

Fortunately, he had only one more delivery to make before he headed back to the Dairy Shack.

As he reached the car, he noticed that the door was open and the dome light was on. A jump rope lay on the ground. Ruthie must have put up quite a fight.

Suddenly, Matt heard a shrill whistle.

"What *now?*" Matt asked Simon, as his younger brother came around the corner from the back of the house.

"I'm looking for Happy," Simon said. "She's missing."

"You can't even take care of your dog, let alone control Ruthie," Matt grumbled.

"Happy! Happy!" Simon cried. "Come here, girl!"

Matt looked inside the Camaro. Then put his hands in his pockets and turned to Simon. "She's right here," he said.

Simon ran toward the car and peered through the window.

In the back seat of Matt's car, Happy was licking her chops. The remains of a hamburger, fries, torn paper wrappings, and gobs of ketchup were scattered all over the upholstery.

Simon turned to face Matt, who waved a second receipt under his nose.

"That'll be seven fifty-five," Matt told him. "And I suggest a very big tip."

As the slow dance ended, so did the spell that seemed to have enveloped Mary. She'd never thought of herself as a mushy, romantic kind of person. She wasn't boy-crazy like her sister Lucy. Mary always thought of herself as practical and sensible in the ways of the heart.

Then came Jordan and this surprising, exciting, extra-special night.

But as happy as she was, Mary knew it was time to end the evening. Slowly, she broke away from Jordan.

"This has been wonderful," she told him. "But I've really got to get home. I think I'm looking at two weeks of being grounded already. I don't want to make that any worse."

"Yeah," Jordan agreed. "Then we'd never get to see each other."

Mary let that thought hang in the air. She didn't want things to move too fast. Besides, there were still Lucy's feelings to deal with. Jordan was her sister's ex-boyfriend, after all.

"I really had a good time tonight," she said sincerely.

"So did I," Jordan replied. "I'm sorry that your date didn't show up," he added.

"That's okay," Mary said, shrugging. "Maybe that was for the best."

Jordan smiled.

Mary was glad the evening would end on an upbeat note. She knew she'd better leave before things got out of hand, and they kissed or something.

She couldn't handle an awkward moment like that. Not tonight.

"Mary! Mary!" a familiar child's voice cried.

She turned away from Jordan as the little blond boy raced across the room and into her arms. Mary lifted him into her arms and gave him a hug.

"Hey, Billy!" she said. "What have you got there?"

"A Red Lightning Superburger Joy-Toy!" he answered, waving the bright plastic object in front of her face. "I got it with my Joytime Supermeal!" he added proudly.

"Wow," Mary replied, gazing in mock envy at the toy.

A moment later, Wilson arrived at Mary's side. He was clearly glad to see her.

"Sorry I'm late," Wilson apologized. "I couldn't find a baby-sitter."

Then Wilson spotted Jordan, and his smile quickly disappeared.

Jordan turned to Mary.

Still holding Billy in her arms, Mary looked back at them, a guilt-filled smile plastered across her face.

EIGHT

Mary tried not to panic as Wilson and Jordan continued to glare at each other.

"Who are you?" Billy asked Jordan.

Jordan smiled at the little boy.

"Hi!" he said, offering Billy his hand. "My name is Jordan. Is your name Billy?"

Billy reached out a tiny hand to shake Jordan's, but Wilson slapped it away.

"Billy doesn't talk to strangers," Wilson told Jordan, taking his son from Mary.

I'd better say something, Mary thought. *Anything. Before they decide to duke it out right here. If that happens, I'll never be able to show my face at Eddie's again.*

"Um, you remember Jordan," Mary said to Wilson. "He's Lucy's ex-boyfriend."

She felt Jordan's eyes on her, and they were filled with hurt. Mary turned away, too chicken to meet his gaze.

"Well, I'd better go," Jordan said stiffly.

Mary smiled weakly. "See you, Jordan," she said with a tiny wave. He nodded and walked away through the crowd.

"Say hello to Lucy for me," Wilson called after him. But if Jordan heard Wilson's jibe, he didn't acknowledge it.

"Well!" Wilson said triumphantly as he turned back to Mary. "Here we are, alone at last."

Just then, Billy screamed "Ka-BOOM!" and tore across the room. He darted between a waiter's legs and stumbled into a table. A woman there jumped up as her drink spilled onto her lap.

Still running, Billy knocked over a chair.

Wilson took off after his son.

"Yeah," Mary muttered. "Alone at last…"

Lucy folded the final batch of clothes. Humming a Top 40 song, she stacked them neatly in a laundry basket.

The washer's bell chimed. Lucy quickly added the fabric softener. As the blue liquid poured into the drum, she thought about her sister.

Lucy had been angry with Mary for the last hour or so. But now her rage was subsiding. She was beyond angry. Now she felt only disappointment and betrayal.

How could Mary abandon me like this? she thought.

Lucy hated to lie, and Mary knew it. But Mary had forced her to be dishonest with their parents. *I feel so guilty,* Lucy told herself.

Her older sister could be so selfish sometimes. It wasn't really part of Mary's nature, it was just that sometimes she went a little crazy. And whenever Mary misbehaved, it usually had something to do with guys.

"Hello, Lucy," Rev. Camden said, entering the laundry room with a new bundle of dirty clothes.

Lucy jumped, startled.

"Um, hi, Dad," she said. She noticed that her father was wearing his bathrobe and that his hair was damp. "Did you just take a shower?" she asked.

"Had to," Rev. Camden said, holding up the bundle of clothes. "Happy had an accident. Which means that these clothes will have to be washed—in hot water."

"Sure, Dad," Lucy replied. "Just throw them in the pile."

"Thanks." Rev. Camden dropped the clothes on the heap. Then he scanned the laundry room.

"My, my," he commented. "You girls are certainly doing a great job."

Lucy nodded, but didn't answer.

"Did I tell you how much your mother and I appreciate what you are *both* doing to help out around here?"

This time, Rev. Camden placed the emphasis on the word "both." But Lucy didn't rise to the bait. Her father sensed something was bothering her, but decided not to pry. He suspected Lucy's funk might have something to do with Mary's defection. *They'll work it out themselves,* he thought.

He lifted the basket of clean clothes. "I'll take care of this," he offered.

"Thanks," Lucy replied, looking down at her hands. They were wrinkled and raw from all the scrubbing she'd done in the bathroom and kitchen.

Rev. Camden paused on his way out. "One more thing," he added sheepishly. "Happy left a little mess in the living room.

"I didn't have time to clean it up and—"

"Got it, Dad," Lucy replied, her nose wrinkling. "I'll take care of it."

Matt glanced in the rear view mirror again and frowned. His tormentor was still on his tail.

Matt knew it was Sergeant Richards in the squad car. The policeman was deliberately following him.

Oh, Sergeant Richards was careful. He always stayed a few car lengths behind Matt's bumper. But now that Matt knew the law was on him, he could easily spot the enemy dogging his every turn.

Matt had picked up the squad car at a traffic light.

The light went from green to yellow just as he hit the intersection. Matt was ready to rush through it when he spotted Sgt. Richards' police car parked in the shadows.

Matt had wasted so much time at home—and then calling in the replacement order for the one Happy had eaten—that he wanted to get back to the Dairy Shack quickly.

But when he saw the cop car, Matt put on the brake.

Sgt. Richards must have been suspicious. He pulled onto the road behind Matt when the light changed—and he'd been on Matt's heels ever since.

Matt was dying to put on some juice and get back to work before Roger had a real spasm. But he couldn't—not with Sgt. Richards on his tail.

Matt glanced at the dashboard clock. *Stuck driving at grandpa speed!* he sighed. *Whatever happened to mutual trust?*

Mary tried to listen to Wilson, but her thoughts kept shifting back to the time—and to Jordan.

After leaving her and Wilson, Jordan had linked up with some friends. Now he was playing pool on the other side of the room. Occasionally, he glanced in Mary's direction.

Wilson talked on, telling Mary about his life with Billy, his time on the west coast, and about returning to Glenoak.

Mary's eyes kept drifting back to Jordan. Finally, he disappeared. Regretfully, Mary returned her full attention to Wilson.

He told her about his part-time job. Then he talked about the parade of babysitters that took care of his son.

Mary understood that Wilson was doing the best he could under the circumstances. But it was a difficult way to raise a child.

How could one person possibly take care of a child by himself? she wondered. Her whole family together was having a hard enough time taking care of the twins.

"I'm thirsty!" Billy announced. Wilson offered him a glass of water, but Billy rejected it.

"Chocolots-a-milk!" he cried shrilly, turning a few heads. "Chocolots-a-milk!"

Wilson summoned the waiter.

"Can I have a glass of chocolate milk?" he asked.

When the waiter departed, so did Billy. Wilson looked relieved. He was having a hard time controlling his son.

"So where was I?" Wilson asked, oblivious to Mary's growing horror.

"Um, your aunt?" Mary prompted.

"Oh, right!" Wilson said. "So anyway, I'm living in my aunt's upstairs apartment. Let me tell you, being locked up with a three-year-old is tough."

Mary nodded politely.

"The place is really small, and it doesn't have a washer or anything," Wilson continued. "I end up hitting the laundromat two or three times a week."

He gazed at Mary, trying to gauge her reaction.

Mary hoped her expression was neutral.

"Usually, my aunt takes care of Billy while I'm at work. But she's away this week, so we guys are on our own."

Mary shivered. It was taking all of her willpower not to run back to Jordan. To fun. To butterflies in her stomach and the promise of a tender kiss. To being a kid.

The early part of the evening had been like a dream. And now it had turned into a nightmare.

The waiter arrived with the chocolate milk. Wilson thanked him, then scanned the room for Billy.

At that moment, the little boy shot across the room, a waitress from another table on his tail. She was obviously angry.

"Hey!" she cried. "Give me that! This is not a game. That money's *real!*"

Wilson got up so fast he knocked against the table and spilled the chocolate milk. Mary jumped backward, but she was too late. Chocolate milk splashed all over her blouse.

Mary grabbed a wad of napkins and dabbed at the mess. Wilson, meanwhile, dived under a table after his son. He came up holding several bills.

"Sorry," Wilson said to the woman. "He's not normally like this."

The waitress snatched the money from Wilson's hand. "Just keep telling yourself that," she snapped.

Mary balled up the wet napkins and dropped them in an empty glass.

"Oh, no," Wilson said when he saw her stained blouse. But Mary shook her head.

"Hey, don't worry about it. It's an old blouse that I don't really like anyway."

"I want my chocolots-a-milk!" Billy demanded.

Wilson tried to signal the waiter. But the man suddenly seemed too busy with customers at other tables. He was deliberately ignoring Wilson.

The people at Eddie's all wanted him—and little Billy—to leave. Eddie's just wasn't the place for a kid to hang out.

Billy struggled in his father's grip. "Chocolots-a-milk!" he demanded.

Mary looked away. *I can never set foot in here again*, she thought miserably.

As Wilson continued to battle with Billy, Mary looked for Jordan. He was standing in a corner talking with one of his buds. He hadn't left after all. But he didn't seem to be paying her the least bit of attention now, either.

This is a total disaster, Mary thought.

The stench of raw gas filled the Dairy Shack's kitchen.

As before, the Three Stooges were fumbling with the gas oven. This time, the one Matt had dubbed Larry was holding a lighted match. The sound of hissing gas was clearly audible.

"I don't think you guys should be doing that," Matt said. "It's pretty dangerous."

"Look!" the redhead shot back. "We *know* how to light the stove."

With that, Larry stuck the match into the dark interior of the oven.

A loud thump shook the kitchen and rattled the glasses. A rolling cloud of fire gushed out of the oven.

Curly jumped backward, falling against Moe. They both landed on the floor.

Larry pulled his head out of the oven,

his face blackened. His hair was singed, and the top of his Dairy Shack hat had ignited.

"Code red!" Curly hollered.

He stumbled over to the sink and grabbed the spray gun, letting loose with a torrent of cold water. It drowned out the fire on Larry's hat—and gagged Larry, too.

Water sprayed all around the kitchen, including inside the oven. There was a loud hiss as the pilot light's flame went out.

Larry pulled off his hat and looked at the scorched remains. Curly looked at Larry, then at the spray gun in his hand. He dropped the hose as Larry charged him.

The third guy—the one Matt had dubbed Moe—whirled around.

"The boss wants to see you!" he told Matt, a look of triumph on his pimply face.

"I think you're in trouble!" Larry cackled, his hands still around Curly's throat.

"Stop laughing," Matt said. *"Now."*

Moe's mouth quickly snapped shut. Larry and Curly stopped struggling.

Matt strode over to Roger Denbro's office and pounded on the door. Behind Matt's back, the Stooges exchanged a meaningful look.

"He's toast," Curly said.

"The poor guy," Larry added.

"He may never work again," Moe joined in. Then a happy thought struck all three of them.

"Great!" they cried, slapping high-fives. "The competition is gone! We'll be the ones back on top of the Dairy Shack food chain!"

"I can't believe you let those three idiots anywhere near an open flame," Matt said as he entered Roger's office.

The night manager looked up. He was sitting behind a tiny desk, the kind they used in grade schools. He sneered at Matt.

"If you are referring to my cooks, I disagree." Roger rose and looked into Matt's eyes. "At least they do their jobs, Camden. At least they are reliable. At least they obey orders—*my* orders."

"What exactly is it about me that's got you all worked up, Roger?" Matt said. "You've had it in for me ever since I walked through that door."

Roger smiled. Matt had to hold himself back from going after the guy.

"That's all in your head, Camden,"

Roger declared, coming around the desk. "I've treated you like every other employee at the Dairy Shack.

"No, Mr. Camden," Roger went on. "It was *you* who abused *our* trust."

"What?" Matt cried.

"Oh, yes," Roger said. "Because of *your* incompetence, we have lost our biggest customer."

Matt shot Roger a skeptical look. "A burger, fries, and a shake is your biggest customer? I don't think so. My family is your biggest customer."

Roger sniffed. "Here at the Dairy Shack, every customer is a big customer."

"Look," Matt said. "I called in a replacement order from my house. I paid for it and I'll take it right over and apologize personally to your *biggest* customer!"

But Roger just shook his head. The customer was extremely upset, and I think we both know what that means."

Matt looked at Roger in disbelief. "Come on!" he pleaded. "Those three clowns out there can't do my job!"

"Ah, there's where you are wrong, Mr. Camden," Roger replied smugly. "Each one of them has a driver's license."

"Oh, sure," Matt said. "But not one of

them has a car. You can't fire me, Roger."

"Oh, yes, I can," Roger shot back. "And do you know why?"

He leaned in toward Matt's face. "Because I'm the boss," he said.

"Man," Matt said disgustedly. "You *are* pathetic." Then he turned and walked out of the office.

In the kitchen, Matt ran into Larry— literally. The red-headed Stooge had changed his shirt and was wearing a brand-new paper hat. He was clutching a bag in his hand.

"Is that the burger, fries, and shake order I called in?" Matt demanded.

Larry nodded. Matt snatched the bag away.

"But...but *I'm* supposed to deliver that!" Larry squawked.

"I'll take care of it," Matt said.

He stopped halfway to the door. "How *were* you going to deliver this, anyway?" he asked.

"Roger was letting me use his Saturn," Larry explained.

For a moment, Matt was tempted to give Larry back the bag.

No, Matt thought. *It's my fault the order got messed up. So it should be me who apol-*

ogizes to the customer. It's the right thing to do.

Just then, Moe entered the kitchen. "What's happening here?" Moe demanded.

"Nothing," Matt shot back. "I'm delivering my order."

Moe's eyes widened. "You're going to defy management? But you no longer work here."

Matt waved the two teenagers away, then walked out the kitchen door.

Larry watched him go, impressed.

"You're my hero," he called after Matt.

Billy seemed a little calmer after a glass of chocolate milk finally made it past his lips. He sat in Wilson's lap, playing with his new Red Lightning toy. As Wilson spoke to Mary, the little boy occasionally smacked his father's face gently.

Finally, Wilson grabbed Billy's hand. "Stop it!" he told him. He turned back to Mary.

"Basically, I'm miserable," he said.

Mary could see that.

"I work all the time," he continued, his words tumbling out. "My job doesn't pay well. And I can't afford all the things Billy and I both need."

Wilson stopped suddenly, and looked into Mary's eyes.

"But the worst thing of all," he said finally, "is that I'm lonely and I can't stop thinking about you...about us. About what we had together, and how I want to have that again."

Mary's heart sank.

Oh, no, she thought miserably. *I've totally changed my mind. This isn't at all what I wanted. Well, maybe it was what I thought I wanted, but...*

She smiled back at Wilson nervously.

He looked so full of hope.

Suddenly, Billy slid away from Wilson's grasp and ran toward another table.

"I'll be right back," Wilson promised.

Sick inside, Mary looked toward the pool tables. Jordan was still there with his friends. Their eyes met. Mary smiled questioningly.

Her heart leaped in her chest when Jordan smiled back at her.

Yes! she cheered silently.

NINE

Rev. and Mrs. Camden paced the bedroom. Each wore a canvas baby carrier containing a crying twin.

Simon sat on the bed. He was marking pages of his latest parenting book with a yellow highlighter. To his surprise, his mom and dad suddenly turned on him.

"What's the idea of letting Ruthie get out of the house?" his mother demanded. "It was the *one* thing—"

"*Two* things," Rev. Camden interrupted. "You forgot about Happy."

"*Two* things we asked you to do. Couldn't you manage two simple tasks?"

"*Simple?*" Simon exclaimed. "Has either of you ever tried to watch Ruthie?"

Rev. and Mrs. Camden stared at him.

"Okay," he sighed. "Dumb question."

"But if it hadn't taken me so long to pay for our Dairy Shack order, Ruthie wouldn't have had time to slip out. You have no idea what it's like…"

"I think we do," Rev. Camden said.

David, who had been calm for a few minutes, suddenly gurgled.

"They could have colic," Simon said, flipping through the pages of his book. "That's a pattern of unexplainable, inconsolable crying that can make any new parent feel like a failure."

As Simon read on, Mrs. Camden whispered in her husband's ear. "Make him leave."

Rev. Camden nodded. He draped the baby carrier holding Samuel over his wife's free shoulder.

"Colic generally doesn't show up until the third or fourth week," he said. "So before you go giving out any more advice, why don't you just take care of your sister and your dog like we asked you to?"

"Why waste a mind like mine on Mickey Mouse jobs like baby-sitting Ruthie?" Simon said. "It's obvious you both need help with the twins."

"That's it," Rev. Camden announced.

He lifted Simon off the bed and hustled his son into the hall.

"As soon as I get some sleep, the little blond boy is *mine*," Mrs. Camden vowed to herself.

Matt checked the address. He was at the right place—a fancy apartment building on Philips Avenue. The building even had a doorman.

"I have a delivery for apartment five," Matt told the security guard.

He glanced again at the receipt, trying to read the name scribbled on the paper. Grease had leaked through the bag and faded the ink.

"Number five has been expecting you," the security guard said, pressing the elevator button. "For about an hour," he added.

"We've had a...a *really* busy night," Matt explained lamely. The guard ushered Matt into the elevator.

"Second floor," he said.

The elevator was lined with mirrors. Matt noted how stupid he looked in his Dairy Shack hat and shirt.

At least this uniform won't be a problem anymore, he thought. *Not now that I've lost my job.*

On the way over, Matt had considered going back to the Dairy Shack in the morning, to speak to Terri about getting his job back. After all, she was the one who had hired him.

Matt also wondered if he could keep his sacking a secret from his father. But that wouldn't be fair. The only way to win the twenty-dollar bet with his dad was to go back to Roger on his hands and knees and beg for his job back.

I'd need more than twenty bucks to do that! Matt told himself. *All I'm going to do is make this last delivery.*

Lucy found Ruthie rummaging in the hall closet. She was searching through the boxes that contained all the baby shower gifts for the twins.

"What are you up to *now*?" Lucy asked.

"Nothing," Ruthie replied, trying to hide something behind her back.

"Fine. You're on your own."

Lucy started to walk away.

"When is Mary going to get home?" Ruthie asked. Lucy froze in her tracks.

"Who said Mary went anywhere?" Lucy asked innocently. Ruthie rolled her eyes.

"I've been trying to get out of here all

night," Ruthie said. "Don't you think I'd know if someone really did break out?"

"You won't say anything, will you?" Lucy said anxiously.

Ruthie shook her head. "Your secret is safe with me," she said.

"Thanks, Ruthie," Lucy said gratefully. "I knew I could count on *one* of my sisters."

Ruthie looked up at her. "Are you mad at her?" she asked.

"Why should I be mad at Mary?" Lucy said.

"For making you do all the cleaning," Ruthie said. "And leaving you behind while she goes out and has fun!"

"I *was* mad at Mary," Lucy confessed. "But now I'm not."

"How come?"

"It's hard to explain," Lucy paused. "But sometimes people you love hurt your feelings. They don't mean to, they just do it anyway. They don't even know they are hurting you."

"Oh," Ruthie said.

"Sometimes people take the ones they love for granted," Lucy explained. "But it doesn't mean they don't love you. Do you understand?" she asked.

"I guess so," Ruthie replied. She considered the way her mom had been ignoring her and spending time with the twins. She also thought of Simon.

"I guess Simon loves me, even though he's a rat who squealed on me."

Lucy laughed. "Something like that."

"And I guess Mom still loves me, even though she spends all her time with those two noisy, stinky babies."

Lucy patted her little sister's arm. "It will get better, I promise."

Ruthie sighed. "That's what *everybody* says."

"Now," Lucy said, changing the subject, "speaking of stinky. I've got some Happy mess to clean up. Do you want to join me?"

"Uck!" Ruthie replied with a shake of her head. "No way, Jose!"

"I know what you mean," Lucy said as she reached for the rug cleaner. "This is one job I would *really* have liked to leave for Mary."

Matt straightened his paper hat and put on his best, most humble smile. The door to apartment five opened.

He blinked in surprise. He saw blond hair. Blue eyes. *Beautiful* blue eyes.

"Shana?" Matt said. "Hey, I haven't

seen you in months! Not since—"

"I can't believe it!" Shana cried. "Matt Camden! What are *you* doing here?"

Matt held up the bag in his hand. "Burgers," he said sheepishly.

Shana smiled. "A working man."

Matt peeked into the studio apartment. It was small but tidy. And very cozy.

"Do you live here?" he asked.

Shana nodded. "As of a few days ago."

Matt smiled. "So you...?"

"Yep," she said proudly. "I moved out."

Matt knew all about Shana's difficult family background. He was glad things were better for her now.

"And your brother?" Matt said.

Shana smiled shyly. "He doesn't live with me. Your father helped him get into a residence program for teens and he helped me find this place."

She stepped aside and presented her studio apartment with a flourish. "So," she said with a bright smile, "I'm here all alone. What time do you get off work?"

Matt grinned. "Guess what?" he announced, ripping the paper hat off his head. "I just got fired. Isn't that *great*?"

Mary lined up her cue stick. When she was

sure everything was perfect, she took the shot.

She put the five ball right into the corner pocket.

When she stood up again, she found herself face-to-face with Wilson.

She called the next shot and lined it up. Another sinker. Again, when she turned, Wilson was there—even closer than before.

"Wilson," Mary said, twisting away. "What's with you tonight?"

Wilson shrugged. But there was a serious, almost desperate look on his face. "I was remembering the last time we were here."

Mary froze as Wilson walked up behind her and put his hands on her arms. Gently but firmly, he turned Mary around so she was facing him again.

"You remember that night, don't you?" Wilson asked. "We came here to talk. You wanted me to say, 'I love you.'"

Mary took a deliberate step backward. "Yeah," she said nervously. "That was pretty funny. I was such a dope."

She looked past Wilson, her eyes scanning the room. "Hey," she said, trying to change the subject. "Where's Billy?"

"He's right there," Wilson said. The little boy was fast asleep under the table.

"He's pretty tired," Mary hinted. "It must be getting late."

"I wish this night had been better. I'm sorry I had to bring Billy with me."

"He's your son," Mary said. "He *should* be a part of your life. The most important part."

"Yeah," Wilson nodded. He moved closer to Mary again. "But having Billy around does make it hard to have a relationship. I guess it took my going away to realize how great we were together."

"Uh-huh," Mary muttered.

She was actually squirming now. She wanted to be out of there. She wanted to be at home with the screaming twins, facing the music from Lucy for going AWOL and from her parents for lying.

Anywhere but with Wilson.

"I'm thinking about coming back to school," Wilson continued.

"That's great," Mary said.

"Well, what do you think?" he asked.

Mary shrugged. "I, um...I guess what I think depends on why you're thinking about coming back."

Wilson leaned into her. "I'm doing it for *us*, Mary," he whispered. "What we had

was really special. I think we could have it
again."

Before she could respond, Wilson
pressed his lips to hers.

His lips were soft and giving. Mary's
were firm and unresponsive. Surprised,
Wilson pulled away.

Mary's eyes sought out Jordan. She saw
him watching her. He'd seen the kiss.

Oh, no! Mary thought.

Wilson looked past her, staring hard at
Jordan.

"Okay," Wilson demanded, his voice
tinged with anger. "Is that Lucy's old
boyfriend or your *new* boyfriend?"

"Nothing is going on between me and
Jordan!" Mary cried in frustration. "And
even if there was, it's none of your business."

Wilson looked stung by Mary's words.

"I'm really sorry about tonight, too,"
Mary added.

"I need to know how you feel about
me," Wilson insisted.

Mary took a deep breath. "Okay, I *cared*
for you. *Once*. You *and* Billy. But you
weren't ready for a serious relationship.
And I thought I was.

"I'm not involved with Jordan," she

continued. "And I don't like being put on the spot to make your life decisions for you. So just go do what you want to do."

"What do *you* want me to do?" Wilson pleaded.

Mary looked him in the eye. "I want you to stop asking me that question and decide for yourself."

"But what about us?" Wilson asked.

"There is no *us*," Mary told him, fighting back tears. "It's...it's all just a little too real for me right now. I'm just a kid."

Wilson looked devastated.

"I really should go home," Mary said quietly. "Good night, Wilson."

Matt watched as Shana shook the milk shake container. It was empty.

"I can get you something else to drink," Matt said, jumping to his feet.

Shana laughed. "Sit down, Matt," she insisted. "You're the guest."

"But as a courteous and efficient driver for the Dairy Shack, it's my duty to serve the customer," Matt said.

"Well," Shana said, "the customer wants you to sit down and relax."

Matt sat down opposite her.

"No, Matt," Shana insisted. "Sit here on the couch—next to me."

The two of them talked for a long time. It had been weeks since they'd seen each other, but their connection was still there— and still strong.

"Are you sure I can't get you something?" Matt asked again finally.

Shana shook her head.

"I said it before: you're the *guest* here. Make yourself at home. You're welcome to anything you want."

Matt slid closer to Shana. "Anything?" he asked.

"Anything," Shana said softly.

"In that case…" Matt's voice trailed off as he leaned over and kissed her.

Mary peeked her head into her parents' bedroom. "Hey, Mom? Dad?"

Rev. and Mrs. Camden waved halfheartedly. They were both sprawled across their bed, totally exhausted. In their cradles, the twins cried on.

"Let *me* try to quiet the babies," Mary offered.

Her parents exchanged doubtful glances. They'd heard that line before.

Mary leaned over the cradles and began to sing her own rendition of a popular hymn.

"Swing low, sweet chariot, coming for to carry me home…"

As Mary sang, Rev. and Mrs. Camden both wondered what she had been up to all night.

But right now, both of them were just too tired to worry about it. There was always tomorrow.

Lucy was back in the upstairs bathroom, on the prowl for dirty towels to fill the load.

She froze when she heard Mary's voice. She was *singing?*

Lucy stalked to her parents' bedroom. The anger she'd thought she'd lost was flooding back.

Mary had just finished her chorus.

Lucy went over and seized Mary's arm. As she dragged her older sister out into the hallway, she glanced back at their parents.

"Could I borrow her for a second?" Lucy said.

Rev. Camden just shrugged. Mrs. Camden smiled. "Thanks for trying to get the babies to sleep."

"Yeah," Rev. Camden added. "Especially after you worked so hard all night."

Mary smiled sweetly. "You're welcome," she cooed. Beside her, Lucy did a slow burn.

In the hallway, Mary noticed Lucy's bedraggled state.

"What happened to you?" she asked. "You look terrible."

Lucy smiled sarcastically. "How nice of you to notice!"

Then she let her older sister have it.

Matt kissed Shana again. They were interrupted by the ringing of Shana's telephone.

"I'd better answer that," Shana said reluctantly. "It might be some kind of emergency."

"Hello," she said into the phone.

"Hello," the caller said. "My name is Roger Denbro. I'm the manager of the Dairy Shack. We spoke earlier this evening, I believe…"

"Uh-huh." Shana smiled and silently motioned for Matt to join her.

"What can I do for you, Mr. Denbro?" Shana replied sweetly.

"I was wondering if you had by any chance seen our delivery boy?"

Shana covered the phone and looked

mischievously at Matt.

"He's got an APB out on you!" she said. "Are you here?"

Matt grinned. "You take it," he said.

"Why, yes," Shana said smoothly. "He *was* here. Such a polite young man, too."

Then she paused. "But I was told that he no longer worked for you."

Roger didn't answer.

"That would be a real shame," Shana continued. "To lose such a valuable employee, I mean."

"You must have been misinformed," Roger said.

Shana kept talking on as if she hadn't heard him. "I bet you can't get that kind of courteous, friendly delivery service anywhere these days."

Matt took the phone from Shana.

"What do you want, Roger?" he asked.

"Matt," the night manager said silkily, "might I interest you in rejoining Team Dairy Shack?"

"Nope. Bye," Matt replied.

"Wait!" Roger screamed. "Please. I'm willing to make a few concessions."

"Like what?" asked Matt.

"Car insurance!" Roger said desperately. "Mileage…and a fifty-cent raise."

"Oh? A whole fifty cents?"

"An *hour*," Roger insisted.

"Fine," Matt said. "But I want the rest of tonight off...with pay."

"But I need you to deliver *tonight*," Roger pleaded. "Thus the offer."

Matt considered Roger's proposition—for two seconds. He looked at Shana.

"Sorry," he announced. "Can't do it."

He hung up the phone and pulled Shana close.

"What about the bet with your father?" she asked.

He nuzzled Shana's hair. "I'll borrow the twenty bucks from Simon."

The phone dropped from Roger's grasp. The Three Stooges heard the dial tone.

"Let that be a lesson to you!" Roger cried, jumping up, pushing them out of his office. "I need to be alone," he whimpered. "Please."

The Three Stooges stood outside the manager's door.

"What do we do now?" Curly asked.

"We've got to take control!" Moe said, drawing himself up. "When management fails, we have to take up the slack!"

Larry cleared his throat. "What do I do

about this?" he asked, shoving a traffic ticket into Moe's hand.

"I failed to signal for a turn. And it's the bossman's car," he confessed.

Moe threw the ticket back at Larry as if it were on fire. "I'm not management. It's not *my* problem." Then he took off.

Larry sighed. "Gee, maybe I shouldn't mention the accident."

TEN

Lucy pushed her sister into their room. "Okay!" she said. "Where *were* you?"

"Eddie's," Mary replied, dropping onto her bed. "Where I said I was going."

Then she smiled. "Actually, it was pretty cool. I got to meet the quarterback on the Centerville team."

"Talk!" Lucy ordered.

"Well, Wilson arrived almost an hour and a half late. That's why I was gone so long."

Lucy nodded expectantly.

"And he had to bring Billy..."

For the next ten minutes, Mary told her sister what had happened with Wilson.

"I'm glad it all worked out for you," Lucy said sincerely. "I could tell you were confused about your feelings for him."

Mary shook her head. "Not anymore!"

Lucy crossed her arms. "So," she said, "what did you do for the hour and a half before Wilson got there?"

Mary suddenly looked nervous.

"You know," Lucy prodded. "While I was scrubbing the entire house?"

Mary smiled weakly. "Actually, it's kind of a funny story. I...um, actually bumped into a friend of yours."

"No surprise there," Lucy cried, throwing up with a wave of her hands. "All of my friends are out tonight."

Then she narrowed her eyes.

"Just which one of my friends would that be?"

Rev. Camden checked his watch.

"It's been ten minutes," he reported. "Should we bust Mary and Lucy yet?"

Mrs. Camden smiled. "Give them a few more minutes."

Suddenly, the entire Camden house echoed with Lucy's angry cries.

"You did *what?*"

Rev. Camden looked admiringly at his wife. "You've still got it!"

They opened their door just a crack.

Mary burst into the hallway a moment later. Lucy was right behind her.

Mary whirled around. "I couldn't help it!" she cried. "I didn't plan to meet him there!"

"I don't care if you planned it or not!" Lucy retorted, hands on hips. "I've been cleaning all night just so you could have a date with *two* guys—one of whom just happens to be my boyfriend!"

"*Ex*-boyfriend!" Mary corrected.

Rev. and Mrs. Camden decided they'd heard enough. They swung open their door. Lucy's back was turned to her parents. But Mary spotted their mom and dad right away.

She tried to signal Lucy with her eyes.

"You had me *lie!*" Lucy said accusingly.

Mary blanched and tipped her head toward her parents.

"I lied and lied and lied," Lucy continued, oblivious. "All night long!"

Finally, she noticed Mary's stricken look.

"Are they standing behind me?" she whispered.

"Yes!" Rev. and Mrs. Camden said.

Lucy turned around. "Allow me," she said. "I'm sending myself to my room."

Mary was left alone with her parents. "Okay!" she cried. "I have to tell you the truth."

"Which is?" demanded her mother.

"I wasn't here at home most of the night. I kind of snuck out to meet Wilson." But I ran into Jordan, instead...I mean, too."

Mary saw no sign of mercy in either of her parents.

"So," Mary said. "I guess it's house arrest for the next couple of weeks."

"*Couple?*" Mrs. Camden replied. "Meaning *two?*"

Mary nodded. Her parents burst into peals of laughter.

"*Two* weeks!" Rev. Camden cried. "You've got to be kidding! That's just a down payment on the time you're going to serve."

"I found out something important," Mary said quickly. "I've outgrown Wilson."

"So all's well that ends well," her father said.

Saved! Mary thought. "Really, Dad?"

"No way!" he answered sternly. "Now go to your room."

Mary blinked. "But Lucy is in there."

Her mother nodded. "Go!"

When Rev. and Mrs. Camden returned to their room, they both sighed in relief. Neither of them liked being hard on their children, but Mary and Lucy deserved what they'd gotten.

The funny thing was, the girls seemed to know it, too.

"I'll say good night to Simon," Rev. Camden told his wife. She nodded.

"Let me just check on the twins. Then I'll spend a couple of minutes with Ruthie," she said.

Simon was lying on his bed, rereading *Twins: The Terror and the Joy*.

"Interesting bedtime choice," Rev. Camden said, entering the room.

Simon looked up at his father. "The crying has to stop, Dad," he said.

Rev. Camden nodded. "And you think this will help?" He grabbed the book and tossed it away. "Simon," he said. "I'm beat. I haven't slept in a week, and I don't want you to take this the wrong way—but you have to stop helping us with the babies."

"But, Dad—"

Rev. Camden held up one hand.

"It's not that we don't appreciate the help," he said.

"But, Dad," Simon argued. "I need to bond with my new brothers."

"The bonding will come," Rev. Camden promised. "But right now, the babies really don't need anyone but Mom. And Mom needs everyone else to help keep this house running."

"I thought it would be fun," Simon said.

"It will be," Rev. Camden said. "I promise."

Rev. Camden ran into Matt in the hallway. His son seemed awfully happy for someone who'd just spent eight hours at a delivery job.

Rev. Camden could see obvious traces of lipstick on his son's face. And he was sure he detected women's perfume.

He smiled. "So it's minimum wage plus tips, is it?"

Matt came clean. "Okay, I owe you twenty bucks. I got fired. It was a humiliating evening, but surprisingly good nonetheless."

Rev. Camden stared at his son. The

babies began to cry again. "I wish I had your life," Rev. Camden said.

Matt nodded. "I know." He paused. "When you said I didn't even know what any job was really all about, what did you mean?" he asked.

Rev. Camden shrugged. "Whatever the job is supposed to be, the work is really to make the boss look good. Does that help?"

Matt sighed. "Next time I'll be a lot more careful about who my boss is."

His father nodded and opened the door to his bedroom.

"By the way," Matt called after him, "thanks for helping Shana find an apartment."

Mrs. Camden was surprised to discover her youngest daughter out of bed and playing with her dolls.

"I came in to say good night," Mrs. Camden whispered.

Ruthie didn't look up.

There was something familiar about the clothes that doll was wearing.

"Isn't that one of the outfits Grandpa and Ginger sent the twins?" Mrs. Camden asked gently.

"Really?" Ruthie said. "I had no idea. It

was just lying around somewhere."

"Yes," Mrs. Camden said, still smiling. "On the third shelf in the linen closet with the rest of the baby gifts."

She sat down on the floor next to Ruthie and held out a large photo album. "I want to show you something," she said.

Ruthie studied the brightly colored album. It had her name spelled out on the cover in big letters.

"It's a baby book," her mother said. "I made it for you a long, long time ago."

Ruthie turned the pages.

"Here's a photograph of you before you were even born," said Mrs. Camden. "See how big my tummy was?"

Ruthie looked up at her mother. "Maybe I never should have come out."

"But look what you would have missed!"

Mrs. Camden showed Ruthie another picture. "That's *you*, riding on your father's shoulder. And here's Simon rocking you on the porch."

Ruthie pointed to another photo.

"That's your first birthday party," her mother explained. "Your brother Matt ate so much cake he got sick."

"Are you going to give me this book when I grow up?" Ruthie asked.

"No, honey," Mrs. Camden replied. "I'm going to give it to you now. I want you to know how special you are."

Ruthie jumped up and hugged her mother. "You mean I get to keep it?" she cried. "In my room? This is so cool!"

Mrs. Camden gave her daughter another hug. Then the twins started crying in the next room.

"It's okay if you have to go, Mom," Ruthie whispered. "I'm a big sister now. I can put myself to bed."

Mrs. Camden wiped away a tear. "Just don't grow up too fast, okay?"

Mrs. Camden pushed open her bedroom door. Her husband was standing there, looking down at the twins.

"I'm overwhelmed," he said.

"Step aside, people," Lucy said, walking into the room. "Give me a shot at this."

She leaned over the cradles and smiled at each twin in turn. Her voice was rich and pure when she began to sing.

"I forgot how beautiful Lucy's voice is,"

Rev. Camden whispered to his wife.

His wife smiled. "And boy, can she clean a toilet."

By midnight, peace reigned in the Camden house. And, miracle of miracles, the twins slept quietly. Lucy crept out of her parents' room and turned off the lights.

Mary and Lucy both lay in bed, staring at the ceiling.

"I'm sorry," Mary whispered finally. "What I did was wrong. I just wanted to say I feel bad about it."

"I know," Lucy said.

"I was selfish and stupid, and I got us both in trouble," Mary went on.

"But at least you figured that out," Lucy replied. "Next time, you'll think before you do something selfish."

Mary smiled. "Yeah, I guess so."

"So," Lucy said, sitting up. "Let's hear all the gruesome details!"

"Details?" Mary asked nervously.

She still hadn't told Lucy the whole truth. But Mary knew that this wasn't the time or place to talk about Jordan.

"Tell me all about Tommy!" Lucy cried.

Mary breathed a sigh of relief. Then she rolled over and faced her sister.

"He drives a BMW?"

Lucy squealed.

Mary quickly shushed her. "You'll wake the twins!"

Both girls giggled. Together, they laughed and talked—very quietly—far into the night.

WIN A TRIP TO HOLLYWOOD!

Official Rules & Regulations

I. HOW TO ENTER

NO PURCHASE NECESSARY. Enter by printing your full name, address, phone number, date of birth, and answer to "What character gets kissed by a stranger?" on a piece of paper, and mailing it to "*7th Heaven* Win a Trip to Hollywood!" Sweepstakes, Random House Children's Books Marketing Department, 1540 Broadway, 19th Floor, New York, NY 10036. Entries must be mailed separately and received by Random House no later than July 31, 2001. LIMIT ONE ENTRY PER PERSON. Partially completed or illegible entries will not be accepted. Sponsors are not responsible for lost, late, mutilated, illegible, stolen, postage-due, incomplete, or misdirected entries. All entries become the property of Random House and will not be returned, so please keep a copy for your records.

II. ELIGIBILITY

Sweepstakes is open to legal residents of the United States, excluding the state of Arizona and Puerto Rico, who are between the ages of 9 and 16 as of July 31, 2001. All federal, state, and local laws and regulations apply. Void wherever prohibited or restricted by law. Employees of Random House Inc., Paramount, Viacom Company, Spelling Television Inc., and their parent companies, assigns, subsidiaries, or affiliates; advertising, promotion, and fulfillment agencies; and their immediate families and persons living in their household are not eligible to enter this sweepstakes.

III. PRIZE

One Grand Prize Winner will win a trip to Hollywood and a Paramount lot tour to the set of *7th Heaven*, including airfare, ground transportation to and from set, lot tour, and airport, a hotel stay for two nights for the winner and one parent/legal guardian, autographed photos of the *7th Heaven* cast, guided lot tour for winner and one parent/legal guardian, and lunch in executive dining room for winner and one parent/legal guardian. (Approximate retail value $1,500.00 U.S.) No other expenses included. Travel and use of accommodations are at risk of winner and winner's parent/legal guardian, and Random House Inc., Paramount, Viacom Company, and Spelling Television Inc. do not assume any liability. If for any reason prize is not available or cannot be fulfilled, Random House Inc. reserves the right to substitute a prize of equal or greater value, including—but not limited to—cash equivalent, which is at the complete discretion of Random House Inc. Taxes, if any, are the winner's sole responsibility. Prizes are not transferable and cannot be assigned. No prize or cash substitutes allowed, except at the discretion of the sponsor as set forth above.

IV. WINNER

Odds of winning depend on total number of entries received. One winner will be selected in a random drawing on or about August 15, 2001, from all eligible entries with the correct answer received within the entry deadline by the Random House Children's Books Marketing Department. By participating, entrants agree to be bound by the official rules and the decision of the judges, which shall be final and binding in all respects. The Grand Prize Winner will win a trip to Hollywood and the set of *7th Heaven*. The prize will be awarded in the name of the winner's parent or legal guardian. Winner's parent or legal guardian will be notified by mail and winner's parent/legal guardian will be required to sign and return affidavit(s) of eligibility and release of liability within 14 days of notification. A noncompliance within that time period or the return of any notification as undeliverable will result in disqualification and the selection of an alternate winner. In the event of any other noncompliance with rules and conditions, prize may be awarded to an alternate winner. Other entry names will NOT be used for subsequent mail solicitation.

V. RESERVATIONS

By participating, winner (and winner's parent/legal guardian) agrees that Random House, Paramount, Viacom Company, Spelling Television Inc., their parent companies, assigns, subsidiaries, or affiliates and advertising, promotion, and fulfillment agencies will have no liability whatsoever and will be held harmless by winner (and winner's parent/legal guardian) for any liability for any injuries, losses, or damages of any kind to person, including death, and property, resulting in whole or in part, directly or indirectly, from the acceptance, possession, misuse, or use of the prize, or participation in this sweepstakes. By entering the sweepstakes winner's parent or legal guardian consents to the use of the winner's name, likeness, and biographical data for publicity and promotional purposes on behalf of Random House, Paramount, Viacom Company, and Spelling Television Inc., with no additional compensation or further permission (except where prohibited by law). Other entry names will NOT be used for subsequent mail solicitation. For the name of the winner, available after August 15, 2001, please send a stamped, self-addressed envelope to: Random House Children's Books Marketing Department, "*7th Heaven* Win a Trip to Hollywood!" Sweepstakes Winner, 1540 Broadway, 19th Floor, New York, NY 10036. Washington and Vermont residents may omit return postage.